T
IGNITE
A
PYRITE
SPIRIT

CALLIE PEY

Dedication

To those who follow their heart with no regard to the consequences, knowing love will find a way.

Special Dedication to Steve for your support while I pursue this dream, and to my Beta Team: Kat B., Jordan M., Danielle W., Ashley B., Emma H., Megan Marie., Allie H., and Hallie H. for your help making this story all that it could be.

Contents

CHAPTER 1 - VALK

Tendrils of red lightning tore across the stormy skies with precision, eliminating obstacles along my flight path. I should have known a different sort of storm was brewing. The clouds hung differently. . .darker, more ominous. . .and were filled with turbulence created by something other than me. Each glide took me lower and lower until I felt the sting of rippling static from the electric charge rolling off the pillowy atmosphere. Lightning and rain often went hand-in-hand. It didn't matter that the sun poked through, promising relief.

But I didn't need liberation from the inclement weather; my magic thrived in it. I was the only dragon here that liked to fly in these conditions. Despite the fire in my veins, rainy skies gave me tremendous peace, but they also created a sense of isolation from the rest of my horde. As if our kind weren't isolated enough, our move to this new world a few centuries ago had left us all with a disparaging sense of loneliness, unavoidable no matter where we traveled.

To avoid any responsibility that might await me in the cavern halls of my brother's lair, I often spent my time in the air, flying as far as I could, searching for something to bring my excitement back to life. Eldates couldn't delegate tasks if I wasn't there to receive them in the first place.

The fire in his veins hadn't taken well to the mundane reality of our current situation. Still, he could roar all he liked about our 'obligations' and 'duties,' but in the end he was the one trying to maintain an old way of life. *Just leave me out of it.* I didn't know what I wanted from this new world yet but following him wasn't high on my list of desires.

Here we had calm blue skies, but above all else, we had freedom from the demands of humankind. *Freedom.* I closed my eyes and leaned into the wind, folding my wings back to dive straight towards the water below.

Before I could drag my claws along the surface of the lake, an icy blast came out of nowhere, forcing me into a sharp pivot to avoid a direct hit. A snarl erupted from my throat. I circled back around and landed on a small island nestled in the center of the massive river that divided our land. Through the mist rising off the water, I searched for the source of the attack.

"I'm sorry, Valk." Izotza's melodic intonation entered my mind. She sounded genuine. *"I was trying to hit Lawry, not you. You just always seem to be in the way."*

As the fog cleared, she landed on the rocks to my left. Her sleek blue form was more suited for swimming, with slim wings and elongated feet that were webbed between her claws. Like most female dragons, she was small, even compared to an adolescent male. However, the ferocity of a female's attack carried an additional punch from the paralyzing toxin they emitted, which made them more deadly.

"I see your aim still hasn't improved much." My retort was met with a scowl. *"What has that ignoramus done now?"* I asked even though I didn't really care to hear about it.

All true born dragons could speak telepathically, but she shifted into her softer form. A blue and white dress hugged her petite figure when she lounged back against the rocks. Her long dark hair was twisted up in a knot on the top of her head, strands caressing her pale skin in the gentle breeze.

Izotza was the only remaining true born female dragon which meant all of the rest of us were supposed to be drawn to her. Unlike the rest of them, I'd never been able to see her as more than a sister, no matter how beautiful she was.

"He's just annoying me," she pouted as she turned her bright blue eyes on me. "I wish *they'd* behave like you do."

Quite a few of the others in our horde had gone through phases trying to pursue her. Fire and ice typically attracted like magnets, so the three remaining fire dragons had continued to try and claim her long after our poison brothers had given up.

A growl rumbled from my chest as Lawry joined us, tossing up more of the fog when he landed on a smaller island to my right. He roared in response to my presence, even though I wasn't pursuing Izo and never had. He was always louder than me, but he definitely was not bigger. We didn't often have issues, but I'd fight with him if he pushed it too far. Fighting for dominance, even in a situation like this where I had no intention of claiming the prize, was instinctual.

My lightning crackled in the sky above us, and he lowered his head in a display of submission that appeased my beast.

His shift happened as quickly as hers, indicating he didn't want to pick a fight with me right now. His dark skin matched my own, and the beige fabric twisted around his waist was accented with rubies and gold to mirror his scales. His shorter cropped white hair blew in the slight breeze from the storm rumbling above us.

He narrowed his red eyes at me.

"What are you doing, Valk?" Lawry asked, sparing a quick glance at Izotza. Was he testing me to see if I'd changed my mind about her? It was clear he was in full pursuit mode. If I'd been anyone else, we would be exchanging blows without even so much as a kind word between us.

I settled my wings against my sides and leveled him with an unamused scowl. *"Channeling with the sky until I was interrupted by you two. Again."*

"Were you flying to the east to finish the map of that quadrant?" Izo asked with a guilty wince, drawing my attention back to her.

We all had hobbies we enjoyed, from books to crafting to hoarding. My free time often went towards creating large maps of the lands I'd fly over. I still had some old maps of the last planet we were on before we relocated here to Artemesia, and my current project was in its final stage. Maybe someday they'd be valuable, but for now they just took up space in my otherwise barren caverns.

"No, today was just to stretch my wings. I'm in no hurry to finish these maps when we have no way off this planet to find new material." I shifted and stretched my arms, listening to the

rapidly racing waters near my feet. I glanced between Lawry and Izo. "Do I need to intervene here?"

While all the fire dragons pursued our icy female companion from time to time, she'd occasionally let Lawry into her space as her one lover. I'd been surprised when she'd chosen him over Eldates initially, but while she liked the passion of his fire, I think she found my brother too demanding. Her selection didn't stop him or Sutenar from testing the waters to see if she'd change her mind. After all, she'd remained unmated to this day.

In this instance though, the last thing I wanted was to get in the middle of a lovers' spat if she was about to nest. Much to her dismay, Izotza's eggs wouldn't hatch, and with each cycle she grew more aggressive and forlorn.

"I can handle myself," she spat, crossing her arms before turning away from us. "He just needs to learn to leave me alone. I think I'm going to hibernate for the next century."

Though she tried to sound tough, raw pain underlined her words, causing Lawry to visibly flinch. He'd tried more than a few times to initiate a mate dance with her but with each unhatched egg, she'd retracted further and further from our small horde.

"I'm not going to just let you fade away, Izo. Let me share your grief. . .let me in."

Yep, I did not need to be here for this.

She didn't reply. She simply rolled off the rock and into the river, shifting in an instant. I didn't enjoy swimming all that much, and the fire dragons liked it even less, so she would usually find some peace in her underwater lair.

Lawry leapt over to our island. Before he could chase her again, I muscled him to a full stop. His skin sizzled against my fingertips, his frustration rising to a boil.

"Maybe just give her some space." I tried to sound casual, but that wasn't our way. Dragons had a way of taking a situation—any situation—and making it more tense, but at least she'd have a head start. If she really wanted to be alone, the entrance of her cave was underwater, too deep for the rest of us to follow.

"Stay out of this, Valk!" He snarled and heat rose between us as flames built in his chest. We couldn't use our breath of fire, or lightning in my case, in these forms, but that didn't mean things would be less hostile. "Just because your soul is dead in matters of the heart doesn't mean the rest of us will sit by while the one we love tortures themselves."

That really wasn't a fair attack, and he knew it. Just because I'd never felt the mating call didn't mean that I didn't care about those around me. I cared about Izo, just not in the same way that he did. How many times did we have to watch her go through the same cycle when it only led her into deeper depression?

"Calm yourself and let her come to you. I think you're being far too pushy. This isn't about how you feel. Think about her."

When his eyes flared, I knew I'd said the wrong thing, but stubborn as I was, I wouldn't take it back.

"I *am* thinking about her! Those were my hatchlings too, but I'm not ready to give up. This land has ruined us, and for all its beauty and safety, we are dying a slow and miserable death. Eldates doesn't see it, but I do. I see her heart break every time she looks at me!" His snarl turned into a resigned sigh. "You wouldn't get it. I don't think you or Velenu genuinely know what it means to love, and to be honest, if we are trapped here, you probably never will."

I pitied him, I truly did, because this could be turning into a one-sided love. He'd be too proud to admit it until she took a different lover. If that happened, then dragon law would ensue which meant that only one of the males would walk away from the fight alive.

"If you are causing her that much distress, then you might already have the answers you are looking for. She might not want to be your mate. Hate to say it, but you might have missed your opportunity."

Lawry roared at me, and his red scales rippled down his skin in a quick transformation. Fire simmered down his elongated neck in preparation for an attack. However, he didn't hold my attention for long. The sky around my brother's volcanic domain exploded in a wall of flames that stretched up and beyond the clouds. In an instant, shadows blocked out the sun, leaving the world around us shrouded in darkness.

CHAPTER 2 – VALK

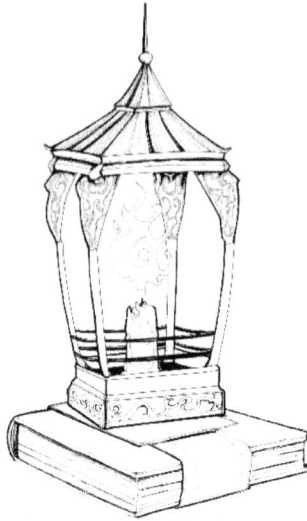

The impending brawl with Lawry was forgotten in an instant as we watched in horror.

What the hell could cause a fire of this magnitude?

Even Eldates couldn't have incited that degree of devastation in such a short span of time. Plumes of ash fell and the heavy smoke dissipated, leaving behind scorched trees and earth as if a volcanic eruption had taken place.

Lawry's shock abated, and he flew over the water, checking for signs of Izotza. But I couldn't take my eyes off the billowing smokestacks. . .and the shadow of an enormous beast silhouetted against the flame-tinted clouds.

No way could a dragon be that large! I was the second largest dragon that I knew of. Eldates and I were the largest dragons here and he was only a smidge larger than I was. It *had* to be a trick of light and flame.

Trick or not, urgency demanded I call upon my beast.

As I shifted, Izotza's blue head popped out of the water, eyes wide with panic. *"Is it the volcano?"*

Lawry swirled around and landed on the edge of the island nearest to her, bowing his head. Whatever fury she'd had before with his harassing behavior seemed to vanish as she crawled through his legs to hide the top of her head along his throat. Her smaller frame was entirely covered from above by the larger dragon.

"I don't think so," Lawry replied. *"There were no warning tremors, and the ground usually moves for days before it erupts."*

"I need to go." I broke the paralyzing tension, not allowing myself to look at the others. Eldates could be in trouble and while it might be a losing fight, I couldn't let him face this alone. *"Lawry?"*

"I'm coming. Izo, burrow into your cave. The water will shield you. I'll come back when it's safe and we know what's going on."

"No! I'm coming with you. My ice could be the advantage you need." She shook the frigid water from her wings, and the three of us launched off towards the explosion.

I galvanized my lightning breath in the depths of my throat as what looked like dark clumps of wind dashed by us, racing in the same direction. Another burst of flames erupted beneath us, the heat of the individual fires fighting for dominance, seeking to claim one another.

In all my centuries, I'd never seen the land so angry before.

A shard of ice sent a blast of glacial wind in my direction. As Izo charged up for a second attempt to extinguish the flames eating the land, I stopped her. Rain would be the only relief for the scorched ground now.

"Hold your power," I told her, using my lightning to draw the distant storm in. *"You will drain yourself, and we still don't know what set it to begin with."*

"I just can't stand to see the earth like this." The sadness in Izo's voice was raw, but she heeded my advice and charged forward.

Lawry roared when those strange dark bursts of wind began to circle above and below us. . .as if they were corralling us. He led an attack of his own, diving down into the cluster. Two of them exploded in a direct hit. The other three scattered, narrowly avoiding being caught in a straight line. I turned my head to the ones above, pivoting my wings just a bit for a clearer view. Unlike a cone of fire breath, my lightning covered a large area. The electric charge crawled up my throat and burst into the air, striking down four of the fleeing wisps.

"They are still going to the volcano!" Izo shouted. *"Hurry!"*

She tucked her wings in and flashed by both of us. I wouldn't be outdone, but the little ice dragon had exceptional speed. Lawry managed to stay on her tail, fire locked and ready to attack anything that got too close.

The flames dispersed from above the volcano as we flew into the sweltering heat. Darkness set upon us, the rising ashes choking the last rays of the day's sunlight. The shadow of a dragon looming in the distance had me pulling back my wings to slow my course. Its head was easily double the size of mine and that wingspan was unlike anything I'd ever seen. Where had this monster come from?

"What is that?" Lawry called out. I didn't miss the quiver in his tone. At least I wasn't alone in the trepidation I was experiencing.

We all took a sharp turn to a cliff protruding from the side of the volcano. The absence of lava immediately ruled out a volcanic explosion. Rain from the storms began to soak the land and snuff out the flames. Steam rose, battling with the smoke billowing from below.

A dark, emerald-green dragon landed on the rocks behind me. I nodded my long neck to acknowledge Otror. Only Velenu was absent. He wouldn't join the fight unless demanded.

"Shift down and enter! You will not use any more of your magic until I say so!" Eldates roared through our minds, causing each of us to flinch at his tone. Why would he tell us not to fight?

Taking a defensive stance, Lawry hovered over Izotza as more dark streaks of energy appeared in the tunnel and blew past us. Sutenar's snarl rippled through our minds. He landed behind me and shifted from his orange-scaled beast. His light complexion was tinted red, made so by his rage at the command of our appointed leader. Smoke poured from his nose as he swallowed the flames of his fire breath.

"That's a stupid order, but I guess it means he's alive."

"Good point," I conceded, taking a slow inhale to calm my racing heart. Everything inside told me that the danger had not passed, that I needed to be ready, but I wouldn't fight a direct order.

A light green dragon slithered up the mountain to the ledge where we all stood. Velenu's wings weren't as large as the rest of ours, and he often felt safer moving along the ground. On his arrival, all seven of us were present.

Between the smoke hanging in the air and the raging storm, nighttime descended upon the land prematurely. The torches

18

along the tunnel wall flared to life, feeding from Eldates' magic and the power in the volcano below us. After nearly coming to blows with Lawry and what just occurred, adrenaline surged through my veins. I marched down the tunnel to the main cavern with more haste than I had shown in years. *Someone better start explaining and soon.*

The man standing in front of Eldates was shorter, but his presence dominated the room. Each step I took towards them sucked more air out of my lungs. His red hair picked up hints of orange from the flames reflecting back at us. Unlike most of us, he wore linens over his entire form. A dark shirt, pants, and boots. Only a peek of his pale wrists was visible between his sleeves and gloved hands.

Behind him, a line of cloaked individuals stood close together, the darkness obscuring any discernible features. Except one. . .their hands emitted a faint glow, all in different hues.

"Is this all of them?" The stranger mused. "Not very many of you left it seems."

I quickly recounted those gathered, and indeed all seven of us stood in the grand hall. Only Velenu hadn't shifted yet, likely his response to the potential danger that stood in our midst. The man didn't appear threatened by him as he took us all in.

The hood of one cloaked individual behind him was lowered.

A woman with braided auburn hair draped over her right shoulder edged closer to the man I could only assume was the beast I'd seen earlier. Fire danced in her palms as she looked around, assessing us.

When her eyes met mine, she dropped her gaze. A show of submission to my challenging stare. My dragon preened at the display. The candlelight flickered off of her lightly tanned skin, but even with my acute eyesight, the room was too dim to catch any more details. I shook my head. I shouldn't have been paying attention to her anyway.

"He's beautiful," Izotza whispered beside me.

I snapped my attention to the ice dragon's soft purring. I wasn't the only one who took notice; Lawry glowered between the newcomer and Izotza. She'd not responded like this in centuries.

"This is all of us," Eldates confirmed with a frown. "However, this really should just be a conversation between us. Your display has been acknowledged. Dismiss your mages, and let's make this a cordial visit. After all, you are new to our planet."

New to the planet? What the fuck did that mean? Hardly anyone came through the portals anymore and not without special permission from the guardian. What was the point of this display of power if they'd gone through the formal process?

"Even so. I'd like us all to be on the same page for the first part of it. Dragon code is different than most, and we all understand the flames, but this is a chance for something more."

Eldates gave his head a slight bow and then gestured for all of us to sit in his pavilion. The six of us moved to follow his indirect command, but I noticed that only the mage's leader joined us. The rest remained at attention in the back, their magic fading until they themselves faded into the shadows along the wall.

Once we were all seated, including the recently shifted Velenu, the man offered each of us a warm smile as if it were a casual gathering and the tension wasn't thick enough to choke a smaller beast. Izo leaned forward as though ready to jump up and run to the stranger if beckoned. Perhaps she was closer to nesting than I'd originally assumed. Outside of his impressive size, I couldn't see anything all that amazing about him. I was lying to myself, of course, but pride wouldn't allow me to think anything differently.

"My name is Aedan. I have come on behalf of my family with some of our mages. We are seeking refuge on your planet as our people have come under persecution for our beliefs."

"Take the mountains to the far south for you and your family," Eldates decreed, even though those technically belonged to Izotza and Sutenar.

Izo didn't appear to want to fight it. Sutenar, on the other hand, jumped to his feet before Aedan held up his hand.

"I'm afraid it's not that simple. We need additional dragons to help us free more of our kin from the bounds that restrain them," Aedan explained. The ease of his tone didn't match the gravity of what he was saying. "Before the rest of them can come, we'd like to live among you to learn the terrain and discuss a partnership of sorts."

"What kind of partnership? It sounds as though you need us to fight for you," Sutenar spat, leveling Aedan with a glower. "I'm inclined to say no unless there is something to benefit us. Giving up my land is one thing, risking my neck is another. And I don't want to do either."

"As a dragon, you would turn your back from a fight when others need you?" Aedan challenged before running a hand through his hair and chuckling. "Things sure must be good here."

"That's not what I said," Sutenar snarled, fist clenching. As hot-headed as he was, he must have realized he needed to consider his words. "Partnership implies certain things. What are you offering in return?"

"It doesn't really matter, does it?" Eldates gave Sutenar a disappointed look and shook his head. "We are dragons, and the fire in our veins demands the fight if there is a call to action. We've been reclusive for long enough." Turning to Aedan, he asked, "How do you propose the arrangements for your people to live amongst us?"

I frowned as I considered Eldates' behavior. He'd just dismissed Sutenar's valid question without any consideration and then rolled over to the next item on his strange agenda.

"It's a lot to host so many mages, so how about if we split them up so that there are two to three per dragon? I'll stay here with you if that is agreeable," Aedan suggested.

My eyes trailed down the line of shadow mages, only pausing on the woman for a second longer than the others. Her eyes were closed as if taking a moment for herself while we were occupied.

"No mages will stay with Izotza," Lawry snarled. Embarrassed, she tried to wave him off, but her cheeks flamed red. Lawry continued, unphased. "If this is the plan, then her numbers will be added to mine."

Aedan considered Lawry for a moment as my fellow dragon exhaled fiery air in a direct challenge to the newcomer.

"That's fine with me as long as it doesn't put too much of a strain on you." He shrugged and turned his attention back to Eldates. "In a few weeks, with your help, we should be able to settle into our own space, and there will be more of us to spice things up on this world."

With their attention refocused, Izo hissed at Lawry under her breath. "Why would you do that?"

"You know why." Lawry leaned back and crossed his arms, refusing to look at her. "I'm not taking any chances with these strangers, and none of you should either."

"You just completely undermined me!"

I rolled my eyes and tried to concentrate on the conversation between Aedan and Eldates instead.

"There are that many females? That could change everything here," Eldates said with a note of pleasant surprise.

"Might be worth mentioning to your group once things have settled down. I'll begin to make the assignments. What are the particular powers of each of your dragons?" Aedan pulled out a scroll and opened it.

"I, Sutenar, and Lawry are fire, like you. Velenu and Otror are poison. Izotza is an ice dragon, and my brother Valk has lightning."

"Strong variety in such a small group. You've been quite fortunate on these lands I see. Most of the other dragons we have are water with a couple of fire. They will be relieved to see your group." As Aedan spoke, I heard his words for what they were: a placation to my brother's ego. And it worked.

Eldates rose in his seat and offered his hand to Aedan. "I'm seeing great things in the future with this partnership."

Aedan clasped his hand and gestured behind him with the other. "One last introduction for this evening."

The auburn-headed mage strode forward. Her soft footfalls made it look as though she were gliding rather than walking. With each step, the robe she wore parted, revealing a hint of translucent fabric accented with black feathers.

My brother, still mid-handshake, froze when she captured his attention. Was that a smile on Aedan's face? Something about her sang to the beast in my chest, but I wasn't the only one captivated. I couldn't shake the suspicion that her very presence distracted us from something very important.

Fire danced throughout her energy, but it wasn't like the flames in our beasts. She was something more than a mage, but what?

"This is Cenara, our high priestess. She'll be staying with the two mages residing with you, Eldates. Cenara speaks with the full authority of myself and my family."

She bowed her head respectfully to Eldates. *Again, that submissive lack of eye contact.* My dragon snarled inside, demanding that I act. That I claim what is mine!

What the hell is wrong with me? I've never cared about anyone else, and now my beast is jealous. . .all because of a stranger?

"Priestess, you say? I guess I have a lot more to learn about this religion you are being hunted for. You never mentioned it in our prior discussions," Eldates replied with the first bit of hesitancy I'd heard so far. "I'm sorry you had to experience such a terse welcome from my kin. Dragons can be quite exquisite hosts. I look forward to making up for this evening and getting to know you much better."

At some point, I'd risen to my feet and moved closer to witness the exchange. Though her smile was meant for Eldates, it teased my beast with the sweetest lure of seduction. This had to be a trap, but I couldn't look away.

Eldates pulled her closer. Yet even though they only touched hands, fire sparked between them. Something new demanded I challenge him right now. Once I won, she'd never be able to look away from my beast ever again. That was how it was supposed to be. That was how I *needed* it to be.

Then she spoke. . .and my world changed, trapping her voice in the depths of my being.

"In a land where fire reigns supreme, if one can't handle the heat of the welcome, they shouldn't be allowed to enjoy comfort in the warmth after."

CHAPTER 3 - VALK

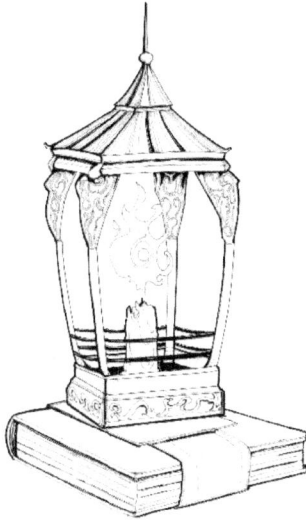

Eldates offered her his arm. I hated to admit it, but her every move was spellbinding. Even the toss of a confirmation glance to this new dragon "Aedan."

Was that hesitation on her part or just my growing desire for there to be an opening?

Aedan responded with a slight tip of his head, and she slipped her arm into the crook of my brother's.

"Come, let's drink to this new partnership!" Eldates gestured to us as he made his way to the volcano's opening.

We often used the center landing for leisurely gatherings, but every few decades the volcano would destroy it, forcing us to rebuild. A series of bridges encircled the perimeter, leading to various caverns. Lining the edges were flora and more seating than we could require for even a gathering this large. Everything was accented with an obnoxious drizzle of gold to mark my brother's importance.

"Why would we celebrate the destruction of our lands?" Velenu whispered. "Did everyone else just forget the fires outside?"

"Fire happens, especially around here." I dismissed his questions with a shrug and pretended I wasn't watching her. My beast senses bristled inside, keenly aware of each step that took her further from me. Why? This wasn't going to go well if I couldn't focus beyond the priestess. The undercurrent of danger lingered in the air. "Observation will be the most important thing we can do. I don't think we've heard the full story."

"I don't want any mages staying with me," he protested again. "What if they touch my books?"

"Then make a statement about it and I don't mean one with words. Make it something that they won't misunderstand." I clapped him on the shoulder and made my way to follow the mages.

Cenara and Eldates stepped onto the rope bridges leading towards the landing.

"Don't be afraid," Eldates teased as she looked over the edge when the bridge shook. "I will catch you if it snaps."

Orange and yellow hues from the lava below cast her face in an angelic glow, captivating me. She didn't appear at all frightened of the rickety pathway or the dangers beneath. Although her head didn't turn, her gaze flicked to mine as if she felt the weight of my stare. Lightning electrified inside my gut. I was desperate to hear her voice again, but she didn't say anything, not even to Eldates.

"He glides while he walks. Have you ever seen anyone move so gracefully?" Izotza's words snapped me out of my trance. Tearing my eyes away, my gaze landed on Aedan. Apparently, I wasn't the only one fixated on a beautiful stranger.

"I don't understand how you find him attractive." Lawry snarled, but she ignored him.

His next rebuttal was interrupted when scrolls began floating through the air to each of the mages. Many of them turned to scout out what I presumed were their assigned dragons.

I wasn't interested in a meet and greet right now. Not unless I got to talk to her.

Taking note of the handful of mages that looked at me, I kept my expression neutral. They could find a lair of their own on the lower rim of my mountain, but if they got too close to my cave, I would kill them all. There wasn't much to my space, but it was mine. I had no issue with establishing boundaries since my brother hadn't thought to mention such things. Eldates and Aedan could claim this was for the sake of hospitality, but I called it for what it was. A takeover.

Otror closed the distance on the cluster of us that remained inside the rocky walls waiting to cross. "Okay, I get it. He made a mandate that they stay and be welcomed, but everything about Aedan seems off."

Izotza purred at the mention of the newcomer, and all three of us frowned. Her icy blue eyes were shifted to slits of her feral dragon lurking beneath, another sign of her incoming nesting. "I'm going to get closer. I *need* to be closer."

She didn't wait for a reply from anyone before shoving past the mages on the bridge and approaching Aedan and my brother.

Devastation flashed across Lawry's face but quickly faded to fury as he fought with his own demons. Without a word, he turned and stormed away from everyone. Several mages separated from the group to follow him.

Is this what we could expect going forward? To never have a moment to ourselves for the next few weeks?

"What is really going on?" Otror hissed. "Everyone has lost their mind!"

I rubbed my chin as I considered his comment. "Maybe so. Lawry's response is the only one that makes any sense. I don't understand why we are doing any of this. Eldates wants to expand our territory and none of the other kingdoms will give us more land, but how can this be the only sane solution?"

"I think it's more than that," Velenu inserted from behind us. "History teaches that those of us who aren't in positions of authority are often left in the dark. Eldates had to know about their arrival beforehand. I can't see him being so cordial otherwise."

Before I barked out a reply in my brother's defense, I thought about his behavior over the past few weeks. He'd been aloof and demanded to be left alone. I'd not seen much of him since the turning of cold winds to spring storms. There was only one thing I could say for sure: he'd never met Cenara before today. The heated look on his face told me that he was immediately ensnared by this newcomer.

"What's his angle then? Why not include us in those earlier discussions?"

Both Otror and Velenu fell silent as they realized I wasn't defending Eldates. In the past, I'd always dismissed any negative talk about our "leader" because I didn't want to give the impression I was vying for the job. It had always been easier if they fell in line behind him. But he'd never done anything like this before.

"I think he wants to come off as a commander who could put us all in our place. He wants the same air of authority that Aedan has," Otror started, picking through his words with caution.

"He's already our named king. Shouldn't that be good enough?" I pointed out as I stepped onto the ledge of the floating platform, making room for them to join me.

"You know as well as I do, we don't follow orders. We're dragons. Not mages, or elves, or dwarves. Last time your brother attempted to give you an order, you went flying to the northern lands and were gone for two weeks. We only came today because we all believed he was in trouble." Velenu laid everything out like a synopsis for the last book he read, and I hated that I couldn't find a way to argue with any of it. "None of this is from a position of power. That illusion will quickly fade."

"Well, we have the appearance of following him now."

"Yes, but it's only a matter of time before something happens. Mages staying with us in our mountains? This can only end badly. None of us want them here, except him," Otror growled low with a pointed look at Eldates.

A mage ran up to them, interrupting the boisterous laughter of Eldates. The hooded figure leaned in and whispered something to Aedan that even my excellent hearing couldn't pick up.

"Are you sure?" Aedan's face pinched in rage when the mage nodded. He turned to Cenara sitting between him and Eldates. "Go and finish it. No more whispers. Return by sunrise."

"Yes, father." She gracefully rose from her seat and wrapped her cloak around her.

"Where are you going?" Eldates asked as she lifted the hood over her hair, blocking her face from my view.

"She shall return. Our old home is under siege, and Cenara is best suited to resolve the matter for my mates." Aedan offered Eldates another glass of the liquor they were drinking. "I could send other mages, but it would take longer for them to complete."

Positioning myself before her, I straightened my spine.

"How about I come with you? You know, in the spirit of our recent partnership." I didn't bother to mask the challenge in my voice. Would they dare to try and stop me? Otror groaned behind me, but I didn't care. I couldn't let her just walk out of here. Besides, wherever she was going and whatever task was at hand could offer some crucial information about what was really going on.

Aedan looked at me as if seeing me for the first time. I registered low on his radar, and my dragon's ego bristled at the dismissal. Aedan and Cenara were only interested in Eldates; the rest of us were no different than the mages surrounding them. I would prove that to be flawed thinking.

"Of course, what a thoughtful idea," he conceded. The man had a curious expression on his face, but I couldn't tell if he agreed with my suggestion.

Cenara glanced at me again but wouldn't meet my eyes. Resignation and annoyance radiated from her. She bowed her head in agreement but then moved at a hastened pace back down the bridge.

"Hurry, Valk!" Eldates snipped at me. "Don't let her fall or get lost."

I swallowed a growl, realizing I couldn't argue with him without wasting time. Pivoting on my heel, I jogged and caught up to her, enjoying the scent of cinnamon and lavender she left behind.

"Do you even know where you are going?" I asked, trying to come up with something to get her to speak to me. Without the distractions of all the others, I just might be able to unbind my dragon's incessant jealousy.

"Yes, I do," she snapped. "And if I remember correctly, I didn't ask for an escort. You just decided to come along." Her tone was clipped, but despite the harshness of her words, my desire to hear her speak more raged.

Her cape blew open, revealing her small, curvy frame as she pulled to a complete halt by a blank wall. A flame made of shadows formed along the wall where we'd stopped, wrapping around itself in a circle. At once, it opened a window to another world. My mouth dropped open. Magic continued to dance along her skin, more shadows imitating flames.

"I know you're not a dragon, yet you walk with flames. Those feathers on your dress won't hold up long to the heat though, no matter how powerful you are as a mage."

Cenara only raised an eyebrow at my commentary, and without looking where she was going, she fell backward into the open sky of the land beyond the rim of fire.

"Hey!" I shouted after her. Scales tore down my body as I shifted and followed. Her tanned skin rippled with brilliant reds, yellows, and oranges. Finally, she twirled in the sky, feathery wings whooshing out to catch her, a tail as bright as the blaze in our hearth trailing behind.

A phoenix. Cenara was a phoenix.

CHAPTER 4 – CENARA

I figured they would find out sooner or later that I was a phoenix and not a dragon. I didn't possess the dominance that a dragon's energy demanded, which could be a dead giveaway the more time I spent around them. Still, I hadn't expected to be outed so soon. Something about him caught my attention, making me want to watch him closely. Currently, I wanted to strangle this guy for his comment about my feathers. Little did he know, I could hold up to the flames even better than any dragon could.

Aedan had been meeting with the dragon king, Eldates, for a few weeks to lay the groundwork for our integration. He'd also been meeting with a few of the fae king's advisors on this new world, but that didn't appear to be moving as fast from the bits of conversation I'd overheard.

While I usually would accompany him to new worlds as we moved before the rest of our family, this time, he'd changed it up. After meeting with the dragon king and collecting raw data, Aedan felt like these beasts would be better assets locked down by the family. My own beast would be enticing enough to draw them into the ritual. Although I didn't love the terms, I'd promised to do my part as always.

It would never be my intention to disturb the plans my family put in place, no matter where we went. My brother's life depended on all of us working in harmony. I would give anything to keep him safe, just as he'd always looked out for me since the day I hatched.

The breeze settled my mind as I sped towards the ground and gave myself freely to the call of the wind. The dragon behind me had fallen quiet as he followed using the same winds. I prayed he couldn't talk to me while we were in these forms. Of course, he had to be the one who offered to go with me. . . The only one who might threaten my composure.

Dragons on every world were attractive, but he was crafted to my preferred specifications. He'd worn barely anything besides his shendyt, as did the other dragons here—the heat from the planet and the depths of the fire in their souls made clothes practically unnecessary, much to my dismay. Golden markings etched over his body had stood out against the backdrop of his dark, glistening skin, reflecting the flames dancing around the room, matching his golden red eyes. His long, wild, dark hair had been pulled back, highlighting his beautiful angles.

I glanced over, noting that the pitch-black scales along his body were outlined with the same golden color that had been inked to his other form. An aching desire filled my body with a need I'd not felt in so very long.

Stop it. I couldn't afford to get caught up in the allure of the beast beside me. It was a distraction I didn't need. I was here to entice and bind the king of the dragons, not to tempt myself on the sights of a lesser man, even if he was breathtaking.

I tucked my wings tight to my side and dove faster towards the surface where Salixa's blue glow radiated from the bubbling waters. I could tell from her trajectory which way I needed to go. She was the orchestrator of His will and the mother of our god. I would always follow her direction.

We'd tried for years to show this world the error of their flawed thoughts and to turn them towards the proper god.

They'd refused to listen, instead turning their backs on His word, and choosing to fight us. Well then, they wouldn't expect the blaze of righteousness that would rain down upon them.

"That's a strange shadow moving across the land," the dragon said in my head. I sighed internally. *"It's not following any patterns that accompany how it should behave in regard to light. What's our mission here?"*

"How about I just show you?" I replied. The temperature notched up inside my body and my feathers sizzled as they transformed into white flames. I'd stand out like a beacon, but they wouldn't have enough time to react. *"Try to keep up with me so **you** don't get lost."*

If he had any more questions, I couldn't hear them as the flame consumed me entirely. I smashed through the village on the first pass, the dynamic shift in temperatures triggering a series of spontaneous combustions. Buildings and trees were splintered to pieces. Fires broke out all around. Wails from the wounded filled the air as smoke consumed the night sky.

"What the fuck are you doing?" he snarled in my mind as I slowed down to pivot back towards the town.

I turned on the gust to taunt him, but my breath caught. He wasn't as big as Aedan, but this dragon was easily double my size. He hovered high above me, watching my every move, his expression torn between confusion and fury. That wingspan was impressive. I used the air current and swung by him.

"I thought you were here to help in the spirit of our new partnership?" I echoed his sentiments from earlier back at him before diving again. I then repeated my attack in a new diagonal, slicing an 'x' across the land.

My brother's shadows rolled along the ground in the perimeter to catch anyone attempting to flee. From the sound of his laughter on the breeze, he was finding pleasure in the events of the evening.

The dragon charged past me, roaring so loudly that I had to pull back and slow my third dive to avoid hitting him.

"What is the meaning of this?" I asked, trying to mask my uncertainty at the posturing beast in front of me. He was protecting them. . . I wasn't sure if I could take him on directly. Brenden's beastly bat form hovered in the distance, but I'd hate to involve the rest of Salixa's mates when they'd called for my aid and were already preoccupied.

"You just attacked this village unprovoked! Calm your flames, we can find another solution." When he wasn't roaring, he wasn't as scary.

"There is no other solution!" I shouted. If a dragon could wince, he did. *"They mean to hurt him, and I won't let anyone do*

that. Choices have consequences, and that is what you are looking at."

"Hurt who?" he asked, sounding genuinely confused. *"All I see are creatures going about their regular lives being chased by flames and shredded by shadows. You are the attacker here, and they are scarcely fighting back!"*

"Get out of my way. If you have no desire to aid my cause then go, return to the cozy keep of your volcano, dragon."

"Valk. My name is—"

Blasts of green energy flew at both of us. Rhythmic chanting, spoken in languages that would soon be lost to time, filled the air and cut off his poorly timed introduction.

Valk roared again and lightning rumbled across the storm-free skies as we were pushed apart from the surge of attacks.

A piercing pain stabbed into my flank just below my rib cage, and a screech tore from my throat. Stupid! I'd let him distract me, and I'd been blind. I screeched again, pouring all my wrath into a fiery cyclone that rippled around me. Though he didn't seem to fear me as he should have, Valk dodged around waves of flames that rolled off my feathers as my fire decimated the world below us.

This annoying planet loved to lace everything with poison. Plants were poison, flesh was poison, even the air to some degree was poisonous. This hadn't been my favorite planet to come to,

41

but my brother had decided that he'd needed a class of warriors that could only be found on this planet. He'd found quite a number of them who heard his message and became devout followers. The rest had been against the rise of this new religion.

Too bad.

These people were among the first who'd been given the opportunity to embrace my brother. . .and this was how they repaid him?

"Were you hit?" Valk asked, flying closer to me.

I didn't miss the hint of a snarl in his voice. *Oh, yes, a big scary dragon is here to save me.* I'd have rolled my eyes if I could, but I didn't have time.

Each moment of delay brought us closer to morning. With the rise of the sun, I'd lose my ability to fly. Aedan had been very clear: I was to return before that happened. If I didn't make it back before daybreak, my life would be forfeit.

I couldn't fail.

With another screech, I continued to torch the land beneath us. When I flew at full speed, I could cover entire continents in flames and misery, but tonight I was supposed to stay here.

"You need to have that looked at!" Valk shouted, managing to keep pace with me. *"Find a place to land and let me help you."*

"Oh, you're a healer now too? Mighty convenient." I pivoted into his path, forcing him to pull back or run into me. *"I think you've done quite enough. Just leave me alone!"*

"I want to understand what's happening here." Apprehension cloaked his voice, allowing me to breathe a bit easier. I wouldn't admit that I was glad he wasn't going to fight me.

"Talk with Aedan. He has other tasks for you; this one is mine." I closed my eyes, drawing power from the gusts I raced in. Fire leaked from my feathers. But the flames couldn't burn away the arrow.

After being under siege by us for more than a decade, they weren't pulling their punches anymore. There was something about a civilization's sunsetting that brought out all of its best qualities. The innovation in this new poison they'd managed to create spoke volumes about their new urgency to fight.

I couldn't tell how long we were out there due to the heavy smoke in the sky around me, but I knew when my flight needed to come to an end. The tips of my wings flickered like a ghostly shadow; the heat seeped from my soul. Turning, I made my way to the new portal that Salixa created for me, guiding me back to Aedan.

"Are we done?" Valk's voice was low as a whisper in the back of my mind.

Ugh, to the wisps, I swear. I'd forgotten all about the stupid beast. *"Yes, I must return."*

"Good, that way I can get a look at that arrow."

Once through the portal, I shifted to my smaller form. I had just a few more moments before the sun would take me away from this life once again.

I glanced around the empty hall where we'd met the other dragons. Everything was quiet in the early hours of the morning. My diminishing flame searched the energy of this volcano to find Aedan's flame. Before I could latch onto it, Valk came up behind me.

His rough hands tossed open my mage's cape, twisting me to face him as he knelt in front of me. His touch trailed up to the arrow lodged in my abdomen. I tried to push him away, but it was half-hearted. His simple caress ignited a heat that shouldn't have been possible now that my transition had begun.

"How were you flying with this? It's lodged so deep."

I hated the concern and fury warring in his eyes. He didn't know me, and he had no right to touch me.

"I'm not so small as a phoenix." I tried to bury any emotion in my words. I knew that in a few minutes, it wouldn't matter anymore. "The arrow wasn't as deep in that form."

"You are still smaller than I am." His matter-of-fact tone did nothing to help the reality that in either form, I was painfully aware of how much larger he was.

"Stop touching me," I commanded, darting my eyes away when he looked up.

"You should stop doing that as well." He chuckled as he rose beside me and took a step back. "If you stay here, I can get the healing stones. We can remove that arrow and clean the wound."

"I don't know what you mean. What should I stop doing?"

"Don't you know?" Valk's voice grew husky. His breath caressed my neck as he leaned in closer. "You speak with me one way, but your body language. . .well, let's just say it's provoking my dragon. You are playing a dangerous game if your words ring true."

"I don't have time for thi—" My words lost their weight as my eyes caught on the rising sun through the cracks of the volcano's surface. Valk turned to face the bright morning light. At least I could enjoy my final view of the night.

CHAPTER 5 – VALK

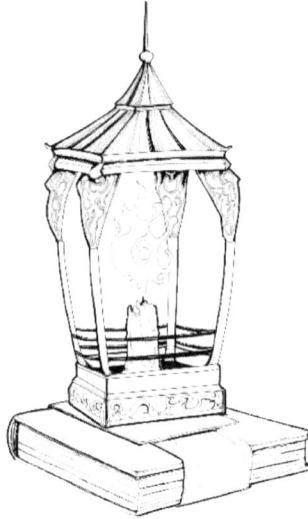

I was remiss to take my eyes off her, but I didn't understand why she was so interested in the sunrise. I thought we were having a perfectly pleasant conversation. Sure, she was annoyed, but Cenara could scream and yell at me all day and night—I'd never been so hungry for another's voice in all my life.

But I needed to focus right now. It was my fault she'd been hit, but I could tend to her wound and make it up to her. In the meantime, we could talk about what I'd just witnessed. If she helped me understand, I could be useful on the next mission. "Yes, the sunrise is beautiful, but—"

I turned, and Cenara was gone. I hadn't even heard her walk away. The warmth of her skin lingered on my fingertips. A quick glance around didn't reveal the direction she'd headed. Even my superior sense of smell couldn't pin her down.

"Cenara?" I called but was met with silence.

Should I be surprised? I'd only been a burden to her since I offered to go and help. After that, I'd roared, blocked, and caused her to get injured. She needed care, and all I could think about was touching her, flirting with her. My chest rumbled with a soft purr as I thought about my fingers caressing her skin. I'd only meant to examine the arrow, but the touch melted my rationale.

It wouldn't be wise to chase her down; she'd clearly decided that she wasn't interested in me. My dragon prowled in my chest, demanding that I pursue her, but I needed to leave her alone if that was what she wanted. There was likely a healer amongst the mages. I needed to forget about the fire between us and get to the bottom of what I saw and what these mages' true intentions were.

After a few hours of sleep, I stalked back down to the landing. Someone had to be awake by now, and I needed to know what happened after I'd left with Cenara.

"Where have you been?" Otror whispered, coming up to my side. "This is madness. Sutenar had a fight with the mages assigned to him. They were all over his cave 'checking for threats.' I thought they'd taken you out when you didn't show up at the gathering this morning."

"Me? No way could that slip of a woman kill me without a fight. Everyone would know about it." I glanced around, trying to appear casual. "Have you seen her today?"

"Their head priestess? No, but I'm guessing you haven't seen the damage their lesser mages did." He hesitated as footsteps approached the far trail but then let out a breath when Velenu appeared. "Where did you go last night?"

"Through a portal to another planet. I'm still confused about the details," I admitted, rubbing the back of my neck. From my perspective, she'd attacked first, but then they'd hit her with that arrow and used magic to attack us.

"Did you see the other dragons they were talking about?" His interest was piqued, and I realized that the offer of additional dragons and potential mates had been the perfect bait.

"No, I didn't see any other dragons." I honestly hadn't taken my eyes off her. There had been phoenixes on Earth before we'd left, so I'd heard about them before. But witnessing the transformation from bird to fire was captivating. "I can't tell if they are the aggressors or the victims. She was injured upon our return. Maybe she's been to see the healer?"

When Otror dismissed my question, I realized I had to let it go for now. My obsession with knowing would draw suspicion. He didn't care if she'd been injured.

"How did Eldates respond to the fight with our new allies?"

Otror frowned again and cast his gaze to the floor. His hands fidgeted, presumably nervous I would take my brother's side.

"What? Tell me!" I growled, immediately regretting the overreaction. It wasn't his fault I was preoccupied with Cenara's disappearance.

He opened and closed his mouth a few times before taking a deep breath. "Sutenar's dragon form has been suppressed as punishment, and he's restricted to his primary cave. No hunting, no flying, no fire. The mages that were assigned to Izotza, the ones who ended up with Lawry, have been added to Sutenar's retinue to ensure he doesn't leave."

"What of the mages?" I asked with caution. Mages couldn't stop Sutenar if he decided to leave, with or without his beast form. As much as I understood how hot-headed a dragon could be, it still took two to fight. This type of punishment spoke to the severity of the situation.

"Two were killed and one is still unconscious. Aedan and Eldates want to discuss this at lunch to make sure we are on the same page." He nodded his head to Velenu as he joined our conversation.

"It's worse than that. When Lawry returned after you left, it almost came to blows between him and Eldates about the punishment." Velenu filled in the rest of the evening's events. "You really shouldn't have gone with her. The amount of uncontrolled fire ego almost tipped off the volcano."

I scoffed, but something serious had been overlooked in all this. We needed ground rules. Boundaries. If I found the mages in my primary cave. . .well, they'd be fried to a crisp. All except one. Their high priestess could touch anything of mine.

I cut off the thought before I purred aloud again. *What has she done to me?*

Eldates and Aedan, followed by a cluster of mages, walked across the northern bridge to join us. I didn't miss Izotza at the back of the group with Lawry trailing behind. My fiery friend's sour mood hadn't improved if his stalking gait was any indication.

"It looks as though we are all here." Eldates offered a smile to the three of us. I returned a barely perceptible nod.

"Are we doing this without Sutenar?" Lawry barked at Eldates, causing my brother to glower in his direction.

"Sutenar is the reason we're having this meeting. Trust me, he knows in excruciating detail what I'm about to say to all of you," Eldates growled, making eye contact with the other four as if I wouldn't be a concern.

Everyone from last night, with the exception of the mages sent to watch over Sutenar, was present. All but one very important auburn-headed priestess.

"One question before we get started," I interrupted Eldates with a raise of my hand. "Cenara? I notice she's not here for this important meeting."

Aedan's indifferent gaze landed on me. "She won't be attending today. As our high priestess, she knows better than to attack our allies."

I opened my mouth to ask specifically about her condition, but Eldates held a hand up. A low growl emitted from my chest, but I decided to drop it. Anyway, why should I care if she went to the healer or not?

"To say I'm disappointed is an understatement. Is this how dragons host company?" Eldates asked.

I couldn't believe he was serious. We fought to take and source our territory. It was literally the only guidance we're given as hatchlings. Once you find your cave, kill anyone who tries to take even a sliver of it away from you. That included the things inside.

Considering these mages weren't dragons, they might not have known the boundaries. Now though, each of them would think twice before entering our caves. Maybe it was unfortunate they tested this with Sutenar first, but I could hardly blame him for his response.

"I expect there to be nothing but cordial behavior moving forward, do you understand me?" he continued as if this wasn't an open dialogue.

"Brother, I think I can speak for all of us," I spoke up, pausing long enough to glance at the others. Lawry was the only one who rolled his eyes. "There need to be ground rules. Sutenar's reaction may have been overly aggressive, but granting access to all our possessions was never clearly laid out. Our personal caves need to be off-limits. Sharing a mountain is one thing, but sharing my nest? I'd have been hard pressed to not respond the same way."

It was Aedan, not Eldates, who answered. "I think we might be able to agree to that. I did not realize that this might have been a territorial response and not an act of aggression about our moving here. We've been treated with such scorn in the past that I may have jumped to a conclusion that wasn't accurate."

I raised my eyebrow at him. "Aren't you the same way with your cave?"

"I haven't had a home in centuries. My mate and our child are in danger, so we move often. But I am territorial with regard to her. We'd discussed that there might be some learning curves, but I want to assure you that our mages do not mean you harm. They merely seek to look after me and my family." Aedan turned to look at the group gathered behind him. "We will have each of the dragons mark their primary caves and moving forward those spaces will be off limits, do you understand?"

"Yes, sir!" they replied in ominous harmony.

"You are dismissed to bury our dead." He returned his attention to Eldates. "I apologize for the interruption."

Something about this whole situation stank. Not only were things not lining up, but he was treating my brother with an eerie reverence that should be only shared between equals. We weren't on the same playing field as this calm monster and yet he was acting humble. *What are they up to?*

"Not at all." Eldates waved off Aedan's apology, and I wanted to gag at the display. "Tomorrow morning, we will begin practice drills to learn how to work together. The mages need to know how to quickly mount and dismount while we are in motion."

My mouth fell open in shock. Lawry roared in pure defiance. "No one is getting on my back!"

I couldn't even begin to try and soften that blow because I agreed with Lawry. I thought we all just had a lovely discussion about boundaries. How was each conversation getting worse? Were these two dragons inhaling the flowers of the groves too heavily?

"We are going to aid them in their quest to reunite their family, and it is easier for them to ride along. They don't move as fast as we do." Eldates strode up to Lawry so that they were eye to eye. "I command that this will be done."

First the order to be mounted, and then Eldates' use of the word 'command' pushed the limits of what most of us could take. Lawry's scales flashed down his skin as he tried to control his temper. "Izotza and Velenu aren't big enough to bring along passengers. The mages got here just fine; I don't see why they can't get wherever it is you are taking us on their own."

Eldates snarled at Lawry and lowered his voice so that only we could hear. "You *will* do this." To the rest, he continued. "It would just be for the larger of us. But everyone will still need to train. We must grow accustomed to each other's powers. This is an important step in becoming allies."

I'd let Cenara get hurt last night because I hadn't been prepared for what to expect when crossing through the portal, so on one hand, I understood what he was saying. Still, I wasn't sure my pride would allow me to be ridden into battle like a majestic steed, no matter what we were fighting for.

"I think you are getting ahead of yourself. It might be time for a chall—" Lawry started until Izotza grabbed his arm. It was the first time in a full solar rotation that her attention was on the fire dragon. It was enough to shut him up.

"Eldates. . .do you intend to do this training as well?" Izo asked, pivoting the attention back to our "fearless" leader. "Will *you* let these strangers mount you?"

"Not you too, Izotza." Eldates groaned, pinching the bridge of his nose.

Lawry's gaze remained on his arm where Izo's hand rested. I was relieved she'd stepped in when she did, diffusing Lawry's fury the moment she touched him.

"I believe it's important to lead by example. We don't know these mages. Half of them continue to mask their faces behind hooded cloaks. Fighting to defend and retrieve Aedan's family is one thing to ask of us, to declare that riders will now use us is another. If we choose to do it to aid an ally, that is true partnership. It's something else entirely to be forced into that position."

"The wisdom of female dragons should not be underestimated," Aedan praised, causing Izotza's face to blush.

With a stern look at each of us, Eldates clenched his jaw before agreeing. "You're right. Let's work on building up comradery. The group Aedan brought with him is devoted to their cause, and I think you all will like their passion." Eldates gestured back to the food that had been set out. The serpentine creatures moved about virtually unnoticed, content to serve us after deeming us their protectors. Half the time, I never even saw them as they scurried around the mountains.

"Not to tip the scales on any newfound peace, but does this mean that Sutenar's punishment can be lifted?" I asked Eldates and Aedan while the others dispersed. "I think we can all agree that last night was an unfortunate turn of events, however, his actions were in line with what should have been expected given the circumstances and lack of boundaries at the time. He was, after all, behaving like a dragon."

Eldates turned to Aedan. Looking for guidance or approval? I considered them both carefully. After a few moments, the tells weren't too hard to decipher. Aedan would come out on top. I wasn't sure my brother knew that just yet.

Finally, Aedan answered. "I don't feel comfortable with that. While I understand that some of it was to be expected, two of my men are dead and are being buried as we speak. Choices must have consequences or else we risk the lesson not being learned. Wouldn't you agree?"

I glowered at him but kept my mouth shut. Anything more that was said would fall on deaf ears. He knew we couldn't challenge him without Eldates on our side. That smug asshole was going to take everything he could from us.

CHAPTER 6 – CENARA

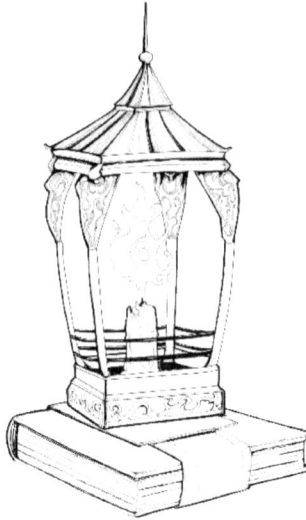

The final rays of sun slipped below the horizon, allowing me to return to the realm with a slow, deep breath. I sat on the ledge of the inner opening in the cavern wall overlooking the magma below. The crimson glow illuminated my skin, giving me what the sun no longer could: warmth. This volcano would likely be dormant for another century, but that didn't diminish its danger. I rather enjoyed that aspect. It was familiar. My whole life had been risk and fighting anyway.

"You were late," Aedan growled. "How do you think He would respond if you didn't return?"

How could I even reply to that? Of course, I knew how my brother would react if I didn't return. He'd devour this world in an angry rage, undermining his own goals in the process. I'd be dead, but it would still be my fault that they were set back another century.

I scrambled to keep my flame tempered so I wouldn't lash out. "The Fursians managed to hit me with an arrow. I couldn't maintain speed. Bringing along one of the dragons before they are fully under our control was reckless. He almost fought me because he didn't understand what was happening! It was too soon, Aedan. How would I have been able to defend myself against an attack from him and complete the mission?"

"Oh, he wouldn't have attacked you. Call it a gut instinct, if you will, but that dragon is all growl and no bite."

"You weren't there! You didn't see—"

"You are being dramatic, and I won't have it right now." Aedan's snarl fell to a forced tolerance as he pulled me off the window ledge.

My recoil at his words caused his scowl to fade into a resigned sigh.

"Did you talk to him? Try to convince him to join our side?"

"I don't want to talk to him," I protested but kept my tone quiet. I was pushing the boundaries of his patience. "Besides, you said I was to focus on the king, not this dragon."

"That's Eldates' brother," he offered, providing me with details that I didn't think were relevant. Brother of the king or not, he still wasn't the king. My orders had been clear, I thought.

"Maybe so, but he's not a fire dragon," I countered as I relived the experience on Fursia. There was lightning but no fire. No charged breath weapon. True, he hadn't flinched in the proximity to my flames, but he hadn't scorched a single thing while we were there.

Aedan raised an eyebrow, considering my words carefully. "How do you know this? I sense fire in him. But. . .now that you mention it, Eldates said his gifts were tied to lightning." A scroll manifested in front of him, allowing him to review notes from the night prior. "An important detail to make sure we don't forget in the future. That would be an extraordinary talent to have."

"He didn't use any of his *talents* to help me at all." I crossed my arms over my chest. "I just don't understand how these lazy dragons are going to help make Him safe, especially if we have to find their treasures to make them compliant enough to get to the altars. Clearly, that backfired yesterday."

"Our mages were careless in a way that you are not. It's fine. Focus on Eldates, but if the other dragons start to get close, don't turn them away either. You need to be approachable to succeed here. We need to think outside the usual boxes. Eldates seems to be willing to lead them all to the ritual without the treasures, so if that's the case, we can close this up quickly. Once we have tied them to our purpose, you can drop the charade, but not a moment before."

If this would protect my brother, then I would do it. Even if I had no clue how to play casual games with one dragon, let alone six. I didn't see this ending well.

"Yes, father," I reluctantly grumbled.

"What have I said? You do *not* call me that." Though he snarled the words, there was no malice in them this time. He strolled out of the room but called back to me. "I expect you to rejoin the group as soon as you've adjusted that attitude."

A sigh escaped from me. Aedan was the most hotheaded of Salixa's four mates. They'd found me when I was a new hatchling, and phoenix hatchlings parent bond to the first living thing they see. Salixa was mine. I'd followed her excitedly from my broken shell before she presented me to their son. Her mates Brenden and Declan hadn't minded when I called them father after seeing their son's reaction that day. Her mate Keane was terrifying, cold, and his attention remained primarily to Salixa. I never spoke to him if I could help it. Aedan hated it when I used the term, but I spent most of my time with him.

Check my attitude, check my attitude. I glanced at the mirror. My auburn hair draped over my shoulder in an elegant braid. But my yellow eyes felt bland thinking about the golden red hue of

Valk's or even the vivid reds and brilliant blues I'd seen in some of the other dragons.

Something crunched underfoot. The ashes of the arrow they'd tried to kill me with had turned to dust. Calling upon the wind, it scattered and vanished.

The toxin never took root, thanks to the fact that during the day, I am nothing more than smoke and shadow. It saved me from any lingering effects after such an attack. While I was spared from death and illness, there was a drawback—we had no sample of the poison to study. The inhabitants of Fursia were getting smarter, but it wouldn't save them in these final weeks.

I knew Valk would likely approach me again once I left the confines of our cavern. How was I supposed to focus on him and the king at the same time? One dragon I could handle. But play intricate courtship games to keep them both interested? *Aedan has lost his damn mind.* But perhaps. . .seduction was the key. *I can do this.* I had to do this.

Smoothing down my dress, pieces of the game wove together in my mind. Aedan wanted me to woo the dragons? Fine. I could be charming, even if it was a muscle I'd never flexed before. I tossed my cloak off to the side before I could put it on. They knew I was a mage. Now they needed to see me as a woman. It was time to pretend to be vulnerable.

I stifled a gag. The whole 'damsel in distress' routine was not my thing.

For all the confidence I felt when I'd decided to leave my cape off, each step weighed me down as if I were trekking through mud. With a deep, steadying breath and a roll of my shoulders to straighten my back, I stepped into the volcano's chamber where introductions had taken place.

Few took note of my entrance. Aedan sat on the far side of the room and tossed me an approving smirk before I met Eldates' heated gaze. His eyes trailed up and down my figure. My breath held firm in my gut while I offered him a shy smile. As I approached the group, I felt more eyes on me, but I didn't give them the same attention. Not yet.

I'd been told to memorize their names, but I'd dismissed the task. Now I was unprepared. Only one name had mattered: Eldates. Suddenly, I needed to play cat and mouse with all the dragons. I should have taken an extra moment to review them, but it was too late now.

The female dragon took measure of me, but she seemed more interested in how Aedan responded to my presence. She needed to tread lightly where he was concerned; he held no favor for anyone other than his true mate, Salixa. This dragon would be sorely outmatched if she ever thought to go up against Aedan's mate. My motherly wisp would slowly flay any misguided love-sick people he interacted with.

"Cenara, how lovely to see you gracing the hall." Eldates pulled out a seat beside him. "I'd have been disappointed to not have your company this evening."

Valk had said that my submissive posturing was sending a message. Did it work on all the dragons or just him? Time to find out.

"That is so kind of you to say, Eldates," I said, my tone sweet like honey. "Please don't let me interrupt."

Before the king responded, Valk slammed his fists down on the table, drawing all attention to him. His expression was masked with something I couldn't quite read as he pinned me in place with his calculating gaze. "I was explaining to the rest of my group what you and I were up to last night. Aedan was about to share some insights into your actions."

My actions? The audacity of this man to behave as if I'd somehow deceived him when I never wanted him to come along with me in the first place! The dark dragon stared me down, burrowing into my soul. I caved under the intensity of his gaze and lowered my head. I was furious with myself for thinking about how attractive he was in the midst of this brutish display.

Keeping my posture demure, I glanced at him through my lashes. Valk's mouth fell slack, and I inwardly smiled. His eyes narrowed, presumably trying to understand my intentions.

Aedan cleared his throat, breaking the tension. "As I have told all of you, we were forced from our home by our hostile neighbors. They are actively hunting my son, so while we would like to get them over here as soon as possible, there's too much about this world that we don't know. Plus, we wouldn't want to impose upon you further by bringing the rest of us."

Eldates nodded at Aedan, his hand brushing the top of my thigh. I forced a smile, though it took everything in me to endure the intimate touch. It made my skin crawl.

"A few more of you would hardly be an imposition. Our lands are vast," Eldates boasted.

Aedan kept his face masked in pleasant neutrality, a feat he'd mastered for these planet conversions. Normally, the beast had only two emotions: rage and passion. I only ever saw the latter around Salixa. "There are more than you might expect."

"How many additional people are we talking about?"

"I'd like to set up our own network of caves before I move them, you see. An area where we wouldn't intrude on what you have built here already. My mages are studying the maps that Valk provided to see if we can identify the proper space."

"Are these the other dragons that you spoke of yesterday? While it's true there might be some territorial disputes, we would welcome more of our kind, especially considering the introduction of some. . .fairer dragons." Eldates glanced my way, but since my smile didn't waver, he slid his eyes to the icy woman in the corner. Her blue scales faded in and out along her skin as if to keep herself cool in this hot atmosphere.

"Are there really more dragons?" Valk asked Aedan outright. Something akin to hope echoed in his voice, and I swallowed down the desire to glare at him. Why should I care if he wanted to find a dragon partner?

"Yes. They will come in time if we can make these lands safe," Aedan promised. The truth was that we did have a few more dragons in our ranks, but they weren't like these magnificent creatures. These seven were more like Aedan, and with them under my brother's influence. . .everything would change.

"There's no danger in our world." The female dragon finally spoke. I wish I remembered her name, that would make this meeting easier. "Not to us anyway. I don't know what it's been like for you in the other worlds, but most of the kingdoms here are peaceful since we left the humans behind. We share a border with the dwarves along our northern ridge. There are also elves, all sorts of fae, and four large groves that share our planet."

I offered an olive branch to the woman so she'd see I was not a threat in any way that she'd perceive. "I'm inclined to believe her. The breeze sings of the gamayun to the north of us. A mythical bird of prophecy wouldn't reside here if there were true dangers. The universe would never allow it."

She considered my words for a moment before nodding her thanks to me. I'd long learned that women would be either my biggest advocates or my worst adversaries in diplomatic matters. Better to get her on my side early if at all possible.

The second fire dragon leaned in closer. "Izotza's right. There's nothing but the usual danger for growing hatchlings. How many more did you say you had? I have most of the mages staying in my mountain. I can look over those maps with them."

"How thoughtful of you, Lawry," Aedan offered with a nod of his head. "The sooner we lock down a location, the faster we can return your mountains back to you. I think that would be the best for everyone involved."

"There's one question you keep dodging." Valk rose to his feet and locked eyes with Aedan. "How man—"

His question was cut off by a series of large explosions on the mountain ridge to the west of this volcano. Right on time. Aedan and I leapt to our feet with the dragons. All eyes turned to the pocket holes in the volcano walls to watch the second round of blasts along the mountain ridge. Flame and smoke danced together in the starry night sky. Internally, I hummed contentedly, but with the flip of a switch, my face echoed the same horror as the others.

"Our mages are out there!" I alerted Aedan in accordance with the script. "They are putting up calls for help."

"I will handle it." He placed a hand on my shoulder with faux concern. "You're still recovering."

"But—"

Eldates' hands gripped my sides. "We will help Aedan. These are our lands, and we need to find out what's going on."

"As long as you are sure. . ." I replied softly.

"Let's go!" Eldates roared after another set of explosions rocked the mountain.

The dragons shifted and took flight into the night sky.

This was the window we'd planned for, giving me time to search for the special dragon treasure. Leave it to Aedan to work around my injuries and twist them to our benefit. Especially when I wasn't actually hurt.

I shook out my hair and took one final look around to make sure I was alone before sprinting for the tunnel to Eldates' cave.

I sensed him long before I heard him. The heat of his gaze and his dominant presence unsettled everything inside me. I'd never experienced anything like it, and I wasn't sure what to do about it. Turning on my heel, I met him head-on. With an involuntary blush, I dropped my gaze. His steps faltered, losing momentum. *I'm really getting to him. It's almost cute.*

"I'm surprised you weren't the first one out that window into the face of danger." Valk closed the few steps between us, his familiar confidence recovered.

"It was hard not to. My mages are in danger, but not all situations are best suited for a phoenix to fight. Besides, my father told me I needed to rest after last night." I made sure to keep my gaze lowered even though I wanted to celebrate how smoothly the lies were falling together.

"Was the arrow poisoned?" he asked.

Was that a tremor in his voice?

"Is that why no one saw you today?"

My instincts screamed to tell him to leave me alone again, but this game meant protecting my brother so he could return to his place in the heavens. It meant everything. Valk seemed like the hero type; could I play the damsel?

"Yes, it was. I am still not up to my full strength. I should have told you last night that I was grateful to have you with me. If I'd lost consciousness. . .well, that might have been the end for me. So, thank you."

"You don't need to thank me. That would have been. . .quite an unfortunate turn of events."

He watched me closely as I took another step closer.

69

Placing my palms against his chest, I slid them along his bare skin with the softest of touches. I hated how much I enjoyed the feel of him beneath my fingertips.

"Why do you call him father? I can sense you don't have any dragon in you. . ." he paused and leaned closer to whisper the last bit against my ear, "yet."

Heat spread throughout my body, my every nerve ending tingling with anticipation as I replayed what he'd said.

I pushed him away and took a retreating step. I needed to get this under my control and fast before he took us in an entirely different direction. "He's not my father by blood, but they found me and raised me." I swallowed hard under the weight of his desire. "I can't take your teases, Valk. Please don't torture me this way."

The ground shook with another explosion as I walked away. He spared just a brief look outside before following me. "Explain yourself. How could I possibly be torturing you?"

"Don't you feel what I do? First this morning and again just now. The way your touch ignites my skin. . .it's a flame I've never experienced." I closed my fists into tiny balls like I was fighting the urge to give into something rash. I turned away from him. "I can't stop thinking about you."

Would he believe it?

Valk fell silent. I hated that I couldn't see his face. Layering lies with enough truth should be the right balance to sell this deception. I wouldn't tell Aedan how much of it had actually been true if I had to recount this story later.

"I haven't been able to get you off of my mind either," he admitted with a sigh. "This is fine, no one here will judge our mating even if you aren't one of us. My beast was just about to demand I chase you until you submitted anyway."

Men. He was taking the bait faster than I'd expected, but now what should I do with it? Before I could process my next thought, he closed the distance. Twisting me back around with surprising ease, he cradled my body against his. I couldn't find the words and simply stared up at him.

"Cenara. This is one thing that you don't have to fight or run from. Dragons are hotheaded when we find a potential mate. If even a small part of you wants to blaze with me, I'm open to a slow. . .and deep exploration." His lips brushed mine, and an unprompted whimper escaped from me.

Damn my stupid body. What had I done? I'd gotten too close to the fire, and he captured this tiny ember of heat between us. What could I do? I needed to slow this down, bring it back to my terms. Terms that weren't real. *This can't be real.*

"You don't understand. Aedan has already proposed my union to the king of dragons. It's in the fine print of the contract.

They are working out the final details. I can't do this with you. My heart would be torn in two. Please, you must forget about this, us. Forget about me."

A predatory expression crossed his face, one that set my own nerves on edge. Claws raked against my skin as scales flickered beneath his. Was he fighting a shift?

"That's not how it should work," he growled, low and throaty. "We don't do betrothals in our kingdom. Mates are the only law our beasts obey. I will speak to my brother and Aedan—"

Well, that didn't help. Dear gods, how was I so bad at this? I shook my head vigorously to cut him off. "No! Please don't. Aedan is so on edge. He wants this union to work. I don't have the headspace to deal with love and mates right now. Remember, my brother. He is the only thing that matters in all of this."

"Yes, I do remember something about that." His reply was slow, and that calculating look returned to his eyes.

"Please. . .just forget I said anything. I'm so sorry to put you in the position of carrying such a burden," I said, the trill of a purr in my tone. I pushed my palms against his chest as I took a step back from him. "I don't feel as though my heart could take it if you continue to look at me that way."

Reluctantly, Valk backed off, but he studied me. I wished for a tiny glimpse of what he was thinking. As much as I shouldn't have wanted it, a new desire built up inside me when his eyes fell to my lips. I wetted them in anticipation of what I shouldn't have been longing for.

A distant explosion trembled the ground all the way up through the base of the volcano.

"Are you going to help them?" I prompted. As much as this distraction had given me a lot to think about, I still had a job to do. If I couldn't get away from him, all of Aedan's efforts would have been for nothing.

"I probably should," he admitted, but he hesitated. "And you are going back to your nest?"

Hmm. That was an interesting question. I actually didn't have a nest here since I hadn't needed one yet, but he wouldn't know that. "Yes. I will await everyone's return."

"Very well then." A deep frown marred the beautiful features of his face, but he gave me a polite nod and retreated.

I waited until he was out of sight before I shifted my arms into phoenix wings so I could dash down the hall to Eldates' chambers. If the king caught me, there was a chance I could spin the reasoning well enough. That weighed on the back of my mind until I crossed the threshold of his cavern.

Gold. There was gold everywhere. The bigger trouble was that I didn't know what I needed to look for. All we knew was that it was special. According to legend, the holder would be able to convince said dragon of anything. Aedan and I hadn't sensed any magical residue from the items that they wore, but perhaps we were missing something.

I avoided touching anything so I wouldn't leave a trace. Not all dragons hoarded items—Aedan didn't—but it didn't have to just be treasure. In Eldates' case, it must have been gold. Otherwise, why would he have so much of it?

My mind drifted to Valk. I wondered what he hoarded. If this was his brother, surely he would also keep a collection like this. . .

No. I didn't have time for daydreams. How one stupid man managed to wiggle his way into my brain after two conversations baffled me. I was better than that, right? After the last exchange, hopefully he would stay away from me until I'd been bonded to his brother. After Aedan seized control of the dragons, well, anything could be possible if I took a liking to him. I'd had lovers in the past, but nothing had felt quite like this. As long as it didn't mess up the missions, I might be able to take him as mine for a bit. I'd have to make that arrangement before the blood bond. Unless, of course, my brother destroyed him for daring to look at me the way he did.

My magic caressed about the room, looking for anything with a hint of fiery magic. With my eyes closed, I listened to the songs of the items. Where would a dragon put their most prized possession? Did they need to see it? Or would they be happy to have it hidden away from the world?

"Winds of flame and shadow, find me what I seek. Enhance it with your fire so I may glimpse it with a peek." I murmured under my breath, giving my mind over to the element of wind as my powers swept over each item in a slow wave so that I didn't miss anything.

"I've thought about it, and I can't abide by what you ask. I won't forget."

I must have jumped three feet in the air at the sound of Valk's voice coming up behind me. I'd not even heard the bulky man enter the room. Turning around to face him, I ended up stumbling to the floor and knocking something over.

Valk's half-shifted form flickered with rolling lightning. Bolts rained down all around me. Magnificent and terrifying at the same time. His furious gaze pinned me in place. If he'd figured out what I was up to. . .I'd be long dead before Aedan would be able to interfere.

CHAPTER 7 – VALK

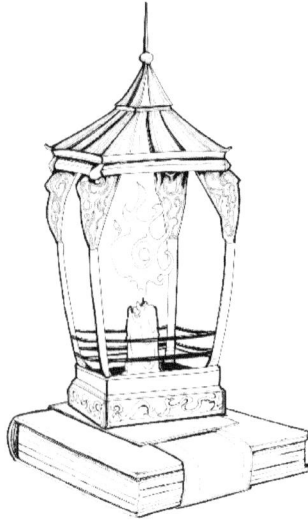

"Seeing you in this room only further serves to make up my mind," I growled, barely able to contain my dragon. "You are *mine.*"

As soon as I'd hit the night air in my flight to join the others, I'd known it was true. If she was injured, then I would care for her. I wouldn't stand on the sidelines as she begged me to forget what surged between us while she gave herself over to Eldates.

Sure, I hadn't thought out all the details. I'd heard stories about dragons finding their mates. And when had I ever seen a dragon's mating go down without one of them going crazy? It was also how Eldates behaved with gold. As soon as he saw it, nothing could stop him from pursuing it. Cenara had triggered something similar in my beast, demanding I have her despite the consequences. She wasn't gold, but she was something so much more precious.

"Valk, please see reason." Cenara tossed a nervous glance around the cavern at my lightning striking the walls before she trembled again. "We *can't* do this. You do not know me well enough to be this certain about anything. I have already signed the contract; we are just waiting on Eldates."

I'd frightened my mate, but I couldn't fight the jealousy rippling through me. Seeing her amongst my brother's possessions, not to mention hearing his name on her lips, was enough to drive me mad. Those sun-kissed eyes of hers watched me warily as I approached. She flinched when I lifted her from the ground, settling only a sliver when she realized the lightning didn't harm her. She didn't fight my hold as I steadied her in my arms. . .her rightful place.

"I'm willing to bet you signed the contract before you met me. Likely before you even arrived here."

"That's hardly the point. Valk. . ."

I loved the way she said my name. She'd used it a few times now, and each time it stroked that place in my chest, warming my soul. Mine should be the only name to come from those perfect lips.

Turning on my heel, I walked out of Eldates' cavern with her cradled in my arms. When entering another dragon's space, uncomfortable prickles broke out along our spine. A holdover from days long since passed when doing something like this would have led to bloodshed. But danger or not, for her, I'd go where I needed to. It'd be a good idea to make sure it wasn't a frequent occurrence.

With each step that brought us further from Eldates' cave, my lightning lessened, and a soft purr built in my chest. Meanwhile, her heart raced with trepidation. I needed to comfort her, even if all we did was talk.

"What were you doing in there anyway? Maybe the other dragons are different, but we are all very territorial about our caves. You missed that meeting earlier."

"Because of your treasures?" Cenara's voice sounded so small, and she trembled again in my arms.

Treasures? Did she mean Eldates' gold? What an unusual question to have. "I'd say it's more like instinct. We are a private species, and we don't like to share. Beyond that, I haven't given it much thought. We have our own space and the space we share with others."

I set her down on a window ledge with as much care as I could. My proximity didn't seem to be calming her. I didn't miss the flinch when I pulled my hand back, almost as if she expected

78

me to hit her. My inner beast snarled at this reaction, ready to punish anyone who'd caused her to behave this way.

"What made you wander in there?"

"I thought I was going to the caves where we are staying, but then I took that last turn and knew I'd made a wrong decision somewhere." She wouldn't meet my gaze before she turned away to face the bright flare of dragon fire in the distance. "Do you collect treasure too?"

Aedan's caves were set up in the opposite direction from where we currently sat. Had she really gotten so turned around? Perhaps she was far more injured than she'd let on earlier. "No, I don't. My cavern is rather sparse." An idea blossomed that probably shouldn't have, but if she was my mate, then she would see it soon anyway. Besides, I could care for her better there. "Would you like to see it?"

I wanted her scent over everything in my cave. My chest let out that soft purr again, and she finally turned her head back to me.

"I don't think that is a good idea. I've already told you, I'm to bond to the king. All he has to do is agree." Cenara glanced down to stare at the center of my chest. "What is this sound you keep making? I've never heard it before."

Even though she'd refused my invitation, I would settle for spending time with her. Especially when she rested her palm against my chest to feel the vibrations of my beast. The warmth of her touch solidified my need to claim and protect her. So, I did the only thing I could think of. I pressed in towards her, causing her face to tilt upwards and slammed my lips against hers. Probably a bit more aggressive than I should have been. I hadn't done this in centuries. She didn't fight to get away from me however, so I'd take that for what it was. With a faint gasp, Cenara submitted, the tremble returning. We exchanged a few kisses before I pulled back to see her face. Her expression turned uncertain.

"I'm not going to hurt you," I promised, kneeling so she wouldn't be intimidated by my size hovering over her. "I'm not going to force you, but I am going to make a claim for you. If my brother hasn't agreed yet, then there's a chance that he doesn't see you the same way I do. We can still sign a deal of cooperation, even if I'm not the king."

"Aedan will think we have conspired against him. I can't. These were the terms of the deal discussed. There is still too much you don't know, and as quickly as you've found yourself infatuated, you can be persuaded elsewhere later. This isn't about mating, Valk, this is about an arranged bond to unite the mages to your group of dragons."

Cenara used the position I was in to slide out from the window and put some distance between us. I hated to admit it, but this chase game was a turn-on. She'd let me get just a little closer each time, and I let her have control of the initial pacing of our dance. I couldn't figure out her real motive, the reason she was so willing to bond to a dragon she didn't know. Mine was simple, whereas hers was layered with things I didn't understand. But not all of it was a misdirection. She didn't seem to like the fact that she responded well to my touch, my purr, my scent. I'd play as long as she didn't bond herself to my brother. There would be trouble if that happened.

"Why us?" I tossed the question out casually. "If you can travel to all the worlds through these portals of yours, why did you pick our group of dragons?"

"I don't make those decisions, so I'm not sure. Eldates approached Aedan when he was here discussing terms with the fae on your world. They have been talking for weeks. Do dragons not all have treasures?" she asked.

I decided to drop it and let the conversation shift. She either didn't know or wouldn't say any more than that. I'd do anything to keep her talking while I figured out my next approach.

"We do, but they aren't what you might think." I let the purr rumble a bit louder, drawing her full attention. The sound enticed her. I'd heard that could happen with mates, but to watch it occur intrigued me. It had been so long since any of us had come across a potential mate. Would she respond to any dragon's purr the

81

same way. . .or just mine? The thought brought up complicated feelings that I wasn't ready to explore.

The ground shook again, and Cenara used the shift in my attention as an opportunity to put a table between us. As if that would save her from the growing heat I saw in her eyes. Those not-so-innocent kisses had changed absolutely everything between us, and I could only think about one thing. Doing it again.

"Explain," she pried, and I cocked my head at her. "Please."

"All right," I conceded, unable to fight the primal need to please her. "We each have one item that we cherish above all others. We may hoard particular items we enjoy, but that comes from a place of comfort. I do not collect things as I have said, but I have something that you could call 'my treasure.'"

She fell quiet for a moment with an adorable scrunch to her features before she spoke again. "Where did you get this one item, and what makes it so special?"

"We are born with it, and you will understand when I show you mine."

Just as I hoped, her expression lit up, any earlier trepidation vanishing. "Do you have it with you?"

This was an interesting change of events. I did have it with me, but right now I wanted to hold her interest. The longer I put it off, the more time I'd have to help her accept my claim to mate her. Lying to a mate wasn't an encouraged practice, but in this case, I knew I needed more time.

"I don't, but I could take you to my cavern. You'd have to wait outside so I can retrieve it, but then I'd love to show you," I offered, but she instantly shut it down with a shake of her head.

"I need to stay here," Cenara insisted, and I forced down the growl that rumbled in the depths of my chest. "Why would you leave something so precious where you don't have eyes on it? What even is it?"

"Too difficult to explain; you'll know when you see it," I replied dismissively. It wasn't hard to explain, but keeping the mystery up would be part of the appeal.

With the discussion at a standstill, I couldn't stay away any longer. I walked around the table. To my surprise, she only took a few steps back. Cupping her face in my hands, I claimed her lips again.

CHAPTER 8 – CENARA

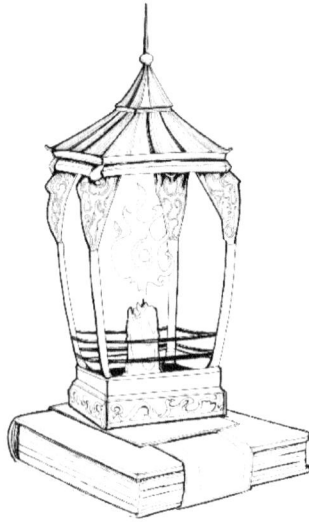

He had to be messing with me. Each kiss tortured me more, struggling between a longing I'd never felt before and the fierce determination to maintain the trap I'd set for him. But in reality, it was so much more. He was a temptation meant only to lead me further astray from my true path. The kisses were tempered, almost as though he was sampling me. Valk was careful not to press too close to me, every move filled with his own calculations. To what end?

I knew what I was after, but there was no way he could have figured it out. So, what was his angle? *Could it really just be as simple as. . .desire?*

"Why are you doing this?" I asked between kisses. But even as I shut my eyes, I became lost in his heat. He tasted like the sun I could no longer fly under, and it threatened to destroy my will to discourage him. "What do you want from me?"

Breaking the sweet teasing, he caressed my cheek with his thumb. "I want you for my mate. I want nothing more than that from you. However, I do understand that in essence, I'm asking you for everything. If that means we must make some type of deal with your family, consider it done. I'll persuade my brother. Just give me the chance. I'll sign whatever you ask. I'll agree to everything you need."

A mate wasn't part of the plan. Not until we'd won the final battle, and that could still be centuries out. The dragons were disposable pieces of the bigger map of the intergalactic war we were entrenched in. My overprotective brother insisted that the blood bond be used so that the dragons couldn't attack me afterward. It could also easily be severed once their usefulness had expired. A mate bond implied and demanded a lot more than that. Not to mention, the death of a mate could render me broken at a time when our mission needed me most. No. I had no interest in a mate bond to any of them.

"I think if you truly knew me, you wouldn't be saying any of this," I replied. It was the most honest thing I'd said to him yet.

"We will have time to learn about each other. Centuries even. I have lived a very long time already, Cenara. I will not waiver from this feeling." His gaze fell to my lips. "My beast knows that you are the one I need to claim, and he's never been wrong."

"Priestess!" A mage shouted as six of them filed into the room. "I come with a message from Salixa for Aedan."

I cursed the interruption internally but used the opportunity to put some distance between Valk and myself. I needed to be away from him in order to think clearly. Valk growled as the man approached. The mages stilled.

"Thank you," I said to the mage as he handed me the rolled-up piece of paper. "How are things on Fursia?" Fursia was the key word for us to use when a dragon was in hearing range. They didn't need to know just yet that we were engaged in warfare on more than one planet.

"Your intervention might be needed on the southern boundary. Our wards aren't holding—"

"She won't be going anywhere until I am certain that she is fully healed," Valk snarled, stepping up behind me.

"You, sir, are not in charge of my itinerary," I snapped over my shoulder. The mage in front of me took a few steps back. We'd never bothered learning many of their names because, much like the dragons, they were expendable. Once they made a deal with my brother, their will wasn't their own anymore, so being polite was just a formality that we often didn't bother with.

"If you won't take care of yourself, then I will do it for you. Either that or you will take me with you," he challenged in return with a smirk on his smug, handsome face.

"I haven't forgotten what happened the last time I took you with me—"

"That won't happen again." Valk cut me off and turned to the mage. "What's the solution to combat the poison? One of my horde may be able to come up with a counter-toxin, but I need to have the base components."

"I think. . .we could get that for you," the man replied, not bothering to mask his surprise at the offer of aid from our current targets.

"Don't get caught up doing things that weren't asked of you," I chided the beastly man.

Valk pulled me back against him with an arm flush against my stomach.

"You need resources. We have them." His chest rumbled with that purr again. I hated how it made my fury lessen instantaneously. Damn tease. "Are we leaving?"

I untangled my body from his grasp and headed towards the window to look out at the night sky tinted with the orange and purples of the rising sun. It was too late for me to go anywhere, let alone with him. "Send word that I will be there tomorrow. I'll pass this message along to Aedan."

"Hail, the deliverer." The mages bowed to me.

"May He bless us always," I replied. They vanished in trails of smoke and shadow as the first flickers of daylight beamed over the horizon.

CHAPTER 9 - VALK

I only took my eyes off her for one moment to watch the mages depart. In my peripheral vision, I could still see her, and without moving, she just vanished. There was no smoke or magical residue from a portal. I turned around in a circle to try and spot her, but nothing.

Unlike earlier when I'd found her in Eldates' cavern, I couldn't track her movements. It was as if she had never existed. Had she gone with the mages despite the message she'd asked them to deliver? The only problem with that logic was that their scent still lingered. Hers did not.

In the sky beyond, the dragons dispersed. The explosions had finally died down, but only Eldates and the massive red and black dragon beside him, which I could only assume was Aedan, headed towards the volcano. They flew in together to the entry tunnels before reappearing in their smaller forms in the main cavernous opening.

My brother noticed me first and gave me a scowl. "What are you looking for Valk?"

"Cenara. I was just talking with her." I tilted my head to look around them. "Did she happen to pass either of you on your way in?"

"Haven't seen her since we left. Thanks for your help, by the way," he snipped, striding past me to the food storages.

"I didn't think you would need me. What would require all of us to defend one territory?"

"Didn't you hear the explosions?"

"Sure. But. . .what happened?" Something in his voice worried me. Staying behind suddenly didn't seem like it had been the best choice. Maybe they had actually needed me. What was going on?

Eldates glanced at Aedan. "Our new allies ended up in the tunnels below Velenu's mountain and ran into the dwarves. The exchange wasn't pleasant, and they attacked us. We lost another couple of mages but took out more of the dwarves in the end. I left Otror to deal with any dwarves who might try to come through. I'll have to discuss this with the world leaders at the next meeting."

He was already speaking as if we were one horde with Aedan and the new mages. "It's official then?"

"I signed the scroll as soon as we landed. The last bit will be setting the blood bonding ceremony three nights from now." Eldates then turned his attention back to Aedan. "Since each of us will have three mages bound to us, should we start collecting the vials tonight?"

"I think we should let the dragons catch their breath after that surprise. The evening will work just fine. It's honestly a pretty straightforward ritual." Aedan shrugged and glanced down the hall to his own chambers. The man never looked exhausted, but that didn't mean he wouldn't like some privacy with how hard Eldates was sucking up to him. "Cenara needs to reorganize the mages now that more have been lost."

"Speaking of, are you able to call her to us? I'd like to discuss the finer points of the agreement with her." The question he asked was cryptic like he didn't want me to fill me in on all the details. Little did he know, she had already filled me in on that clause.

I wanted to interject, but Aedan replied, cutting me off. "I do, but she had another matter to attend to, and then she needs to rest for the day. That conversation will also have to wait for tonight, I'm afraid. She's going to be quite a busy priestess when she returns."

My brother only nodded his head, but that didn't sound right to me. Phoenixes were made of fire in their essence, just like most dragons. While I could stay up through the night, my power was enhanced by the sun, as hers should be too.

"Then it shall wait. I'd like this to be finalized so that we can get the rest of your family relocated quickly. Once they are settled, we can discuss the additional dragons."

"Brother, may I speak with you privately?" I implored. I couldn't lose her, and I wasn't willing to believe that a scroll couldn't be altered.

"I will not be persuaded away from the agreement we have signed, Valk. Whatever you need to say can be said in front of Aedan. He's a fellow dragon, our goals are in alignment with each other."

"Eldates, I'm not asking to refuse the agreement. If possible, I would like to request Cenara be bonded or mated to me," I offered. No one moved, but I caught the calculation in Aedan's eyes. "I've been thinking about it, and we might want to keep your options open for the other dragons. I can do this in your stead."

"Is that why you stayed behind?" Eldates snarled at me. "Are you scheming to usurp my position while the rest of us fight in the depths? I'm always cleaning up after you and now this in front of our distinguished guest?"

I wanted to snarl at his reaction, but navigating this with Cenara would prove to be difficult enough if I didn't control my temper. "Of course not, Eldates. Her fire sparks mine, and I think she might be my mate," I answered honestly to temper his flame. "I haven't moved to claim her. I thought I might have time to discuss it with you both, but the changes are happening rapidly."

"Mate?" Eldates considered me, and then he laughed. "There's no way that mage is your mate. She's not even a dragon. No. Cenara will be blood bound to me, but don't fret, little brother, we can work something out."

That asshole was mocking me. "There's nothing to work out. I'm doing you a courtesy by coming to you this way."

Aedan turned to speak with three mages who'd just walked in. He was clearly uninterested in our discussion over his high priestess. I growled low in my chest when Eldates grabbed my elbow and guided me further away from Aedan.

"Calm your anger, Valk. No one has to do a mating dance with her. I've looked over the terms, and that isn't a requirement. She'll just be ours." He kept his voice low, but I heard every word. "You fancy her? Then I'll gift her to you and any of the others that do well with our coming battles. More dragons are coming, and that is why we need to be patient. She is of no consequence after we secure our place in their ranks. Do you understand me?"

"You don't intend to mate her?" I asked, making sure I followed what he was saying.

"No, of course not. Once I've had my fun, you can take her for as long as you want. My only caveat is that I need you on board moving forward. You need to act like I am your king."

He watched me knowingly, and I. . .I'd walked straight into that trap. Damn it! I'd fucking handed him the information he needed to wrangle me under his control. What was it about this woman that wound my brain up this way?

"What does he think is happening?" I gave the slightest nod in Aedan's direction.

"That I am bonding to her per the deal. She's their priestess, and I'm the king. The blood bond is part of the deal regardless of the mage. They will be granted some of our magic, and we will get their undying oath of loyalty. They will live and breathe for us."

"Cenara doesn't need your power." She was a brutal force of fire and wind. When unleashed, she could bring civilizations to their knees. I'd seen it already. What could Eldates give her that she didn't already have? For the other mages, I could see why they would agree to this, but her? What did *she* stand to gain?

"Maybe not, but I will have her unrelenting loyalty. She will worship the ground I walk on, and if I give her a command, she will obey."

I suppressed my urge to reply, but there was still one thing I needed answers to. "How long have you been planning with them? I understand the move for more power, but there has to be more than that."

"Some things you have to take on faith, Valk. I have been working for our best interests. We moved to get away from the humans and to claim new lands, but we're stifled here. With their resources, everything is open to us. We just have to play along for a bit." He lowered his voice. "The others won't fight this transition if you don't. Trust me. Whatever nonsense this ritual is, it will be worth it."

CHAPTER 10 – CENARA

Sliding down from the perch where I'd been watching the day's events, I enjoyed the tingle of magic against my skin as my body manifested itself back into existence. It was hard to spend my days this way, but nothing would change it—not until my brother was free from the chains that limited His power. Only he could cure me, and until then, I was bound to repeat this cycle indefinitely.

Hair stood on end along my skin, warning me of danger just before my throat was caught in a tight grip that I knew all too well. Aedan lifted me off the ground. I tried in vain to pry his fingers back, my feet flailing.

He snarled, his hot breath spreading across my cheek as he pulled me in close so no one else would hear. "What the fuck are you doing? Are you plotting against us?"

I tried to answer but nothing except a creak of air would escape. His fingers dug deeper into my skin, his clamp on my windpipe less than the force he needed to crush it, but just barely.

Wide-eyed, I shook my head as vigorously as I could. He was going to kill me, and there would be no way for me to stop him.

Black spots blurred my vision. I gasped; the sharp intake of breath was all I could muster. This couldn't be his true intent. If Aedan wanted me dead, he could simply release the anchor that my flame latched onto during the day. I wouldn't be able to do anything to stop him. No. He meant to get information through punishing me. Why? What had I done wrong?

A deep growl rumbled in his chest. Using all the power of his locked beast, he flung me into the stone wall. My hollow bones shattered along my side when I landed on the ground wrong.

I knew better than to make eye contact with him again. Gasping to catch my breath, I ignored the pain screaming throughout my body. Struggling to sit up, I got on my knees, head bowed, my hands on the ground in front of me. In the past, he'd broken almost every bone in my body. He wouldn't hesitate to do it again. My brother didn't have time for me to fail him now, and it wouldn't matter if Aedan's brutality was the reason for my delay.

"Mate? Did you plant this idea?" Aedan demanded.

Mate? I echoed internally, searching my memory for anything that could have triggered this type of response. The only thing I could think of was Valk. What had that stupid dragon said?

"I have no mate. I don't know what you're talking about. I do as you say, always. I am not plotting. Valk found me looking for the treasure in the king's caves. That's all. Please, Father. I promise."

"Do not call me that. What have you told him?" he snarled, stepping closer.

I held my breath, praying he wouldn't grab me again.

"Nothing. I swear it. He's been obsessively following me. I am leading him on for information like you told me to do. That's it. I was trying to be approachable, but I think he took it to mean more." I stumbled over my words, desperate to see Aedan's expression. Instead, I stared at the cut of the rocks that made up the cavern floor. Sharp jolts of pain rippled up and down my body as it protested staying in a crouched position.

"Well? Did he give you anything useful?" He pressed but otherwise didn't move.

"The items we are looking for are something they are born with. He's offered to show me his treasure."

"In exchange for what?"

Everything hurt, making it difficult to recount the conversation with Valk in my mind. *Leave out the kisses; Aedan won't care about that. Or worse, he might take it as further betrayal.*

"I have to go to his cave. He didn't have it on him. I refused yesterday because I didn't want to abandon my post, but then he wouldn't leave me alone. Eldates' chamber is full of gold. It will take time to find it, but I can't do anything if Valk is stalking behind me every step of the way."

Silence. Aedan left me hanging in that horrifying silence, and I could do nothing to change it. I could only wait with bated breath to see if the fury of his flame receded.

His fire wasn't like mine. Mine sang to me like warmth in the pit of my stomach, a caress from the softest blanket on the coldest night of the year. Aedan's made my skin crawl with an urgent need to run and never look back. Like if I did, I would be burned to an ash I could never rise from. Like his flames would consume everything, rendering my soul completely gone.

My body trembled with pain, and bruises bloomed down my right side. With his slight exhale to regulate his fury, I knew he decided to spare me. Today, anyway.

"Keeping him ensnared could play to our favor before the blood bonding. That was quick thinking. Rise, Cenara."

Though my hands shook as I lifted myself off the floor, I met his gaze with gratitude. Keeping all my weight on my left foot provided some relief to my loosely attached right ankle. Aedan tilted my head up, examining the marks he'd likely left on my throat. And though he frowned, he gestured for me to take a seat before handing me a vial of Salixa's potion. She'd made extra for this trip. Without Brenden to intervene, we figured it might get rough for me because of Aedan's raw aggression.

The potion was a thick blue liquid and tasted like rotten flesh, but the effects were instantaneous. The cool relief refreshed my body; it was as if the encounter had never even happened. I envied Salixa's magic and was thankful she'd been so considerate when she didn't have to be.

"That's better. Can't have the bait looking anything but perfect in the final negotiations." Aedan nodded his head at the vanishing bruises. "Are you able to navigate a game with both of them?"

"Both?" I eyed him with caution. I hadn't intended to fully play a game with Valk while acquiring his treasure. Sure, I enjoyed the way he kissed me and even the slight hint of obsession that I'd picked up on, but my mission was the king.

"Yes. With what transpired earlier between Eldates and his brother, Eldates may not be strong enough to control his people." Aedan leaned back in the seat he'd taken. "I'm not willing to put all our efforts into any one particular dragon just yet. If you can cause Valk to snap, get him to display a higher ability than Eldates, he may be the dragon we need."

"But what about the treaty terms? I thought that was set in stone now that the scroll has been signed?"

Aedan *tsked* at me and shook his head. "You're smarter than that. The blood bond is between the king and the high priestess. Both positions can easily have the player exchanged. We need you to control the most powerful dragon. If that's not the current king, he can be removed."

A tingle of fear ran down my spine. I straightened and asked, "If I can get the treasures from the dragons, then we won't have to go through with the bonding at all, right? Better to save it for later if we need it."

"Cenara. We discussed this. These are not our usual acquisitions; *He* needs you to have the dragons under your full control. The treasures will simply give us the ability to speak through the dragons before the blood ritual and after that, to the lesser reptile beasts here. The blood bonding is happening regardless. We cannot have a shadow of doubt that they will do as they are commanded in the coming battles." Aedan released an amused chuckle that was neither warm nor friendly. "The best thing is, after the bonding, you won't have to endure any more of their handsy behavior. They will be no better than beasts without willpower."

It took everything I had not to groan. I couldn't get out of this bonding. But for my brother, I would do it; I wouldn't deny Him anything.

"I will continue to seek out the items then and prepare for the ritual. Please know this fact, Aedan—I will never betray him. Until he emerges from the shadows as the true and rightful god he is, you will always be able to count on me."

CHAPTER 11 – VALK

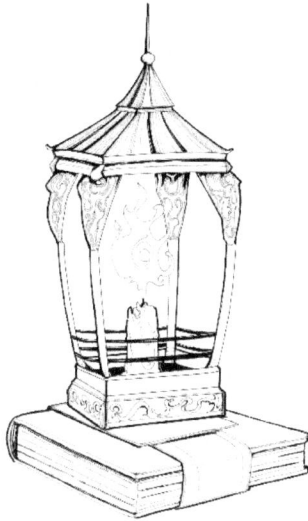

I couldn't smell her anywhere during the day, and it drove me to madness. I knew she was here. My dragon beast screamed at me to find her and make sure she was safe. Hide her in our cave so nothing could harm her.

That wasn't practical. Namely, she wasn't in any danger here in Eldates' volcano. There was nothing that hunted us in the dragon lands, so why would she need protection? We were the biggest creatures, and with my senses, I'd know if there was a stranger here. Not to mention, I was pretty confident that she could protect herself from lesser beasts.

As soon as the sun slipped under the horizon line, her scent returned. Inside the chambers that Aedan now claimed for his own. How had she managed to slip by all of us? Magic was limited inside the caverns; we didn't want any of our treasures to be stolen. There was no way the mages were more powerful than our innate gifts protecting our lairs.

The beast inside urged me to go to her now that we knew where she was. But I needed to be patient, see how this played out with my brother. Could I stand by and just wait for my turn? Could I let Eldates blood bond her and be okay with waiting for him to hand her over? What if he took her back from me?

Cenara strode out of the cavern hall looking like an absolute vision. The dress billowed in the breeze she created, offering teases of her smooth legs through the slits; her auburn hair blew back off her shoulder. She did a quick once-over to see who else was in the room. Her eyes met mine first. Though a small smile tugged on her lips, she turned away and approached my brother.

"I've heard that good news is in order," she said, dipping her head low in a greeting.

Eldates flicked his gaze to me, gauging how I would behave. With the knowledge that I wished to claim her as mine, his touch could put us in a precarious situation. He took her hand and pulled her in closer, indicating for her to take a seat beside him.

This was a test to see if I would comply with his directive. Fury burned through me, but it wasn't his intentions that tormented me. It was the smile on her face, directed at him. The warmth of the gift she offered him when she didn't understand how he intended to use her. I snarled and stormed out of the cavern without another look back. I had a few days to figure out if I would be willing to go along with Eldates' plan or if I would have to do as my beast demanded. I needed to leave now while I still had some semblance of control.

Could she truly ignore the passion, our kiss, the sizzle that sparked between us when we touched? Lightning crackled off of me as I stormed towards the exit of Eldates' volcano. I needed to fly off this new anger. I couldn't forget anything; I'd told her that, and I meant it. I just didn't understand where this obsession had come from. Every part of me demanded I go back in there and take her away. She was enigmatic and beautiful, but more than that, she was mine.

The night sky beckoned me to escape all my worries, just like I'd been doing all my life. I'd never spent so much time inside before, couldn't stand being with my arrogant brother.

In the past, I could have taken control of the horde, but I'd been aloof and disinterested. With no kingdoms to ransack and plenty of food to eat, we'd never needed anything. It had led to a mundane existence full of bland memories that extended through the centuries. This was why some dragons preferred to sleep for centuries, waiting for that next big pursuit. None of us had done that here yet, but it was a topic of conversation from time to time.

A small sniffle came from my left. I followed it around to the rocky ledge on the side of the entrance and found Izo. Her legs dangled over the edge as she sat hunched over. Trails of tears rolled down her cheeks.

"Are you crying?" I asked, perhaps a bit more gruffly than intended, but it was so out of character. "Did Lawry hurt you?" If needed, I would pick a fight with him tonight just to make both of us feel better.

She flinched at the sound of my voice, swiping her face dry. "No. It's not about Lawry." She shook her head, taking a deep breath. "He won't even acknowledge me. I don't know what to do."

If it wasn't about Lawry, then she had to be talking about Aedan. She'd been following him like a lost hatchling since he'd arrived. We all had noticed it.

"Izo, you know he's mated already," I offered, crouching down to sit beside her. "You wouldn't want your mate to pay any attention to another dragon, no matter how perfect she is. This is the path of our people."

"Then she's no dragon," she spat out with disgust, fresh tears falling down her cheeks. "I cannot sense her. Why is she not with him?"

"She's coming over with their son when Aedan feels it's safe. I don't think she is a dragon, but you know that not all our mates will be." I tried to rationalize but then realized she probably didn't give a damn about what I had to say. I wrapped my arm around her, and she crumpled into my chest crying. Nothing doused a fire faster than a woman's heartbreak, especially one you consider a sister. I stroked her hair and wondered how I could turn this around. "Hey, what do you think the other dragons will be like?"

The distraction worked. The flow of her tears slowed; her shaking shoulders relaxed. "I can't even imagine them, honestly. How long has it been just us? What if we don't get along with them?"

I had thought about that as well. New dragons usually meant a fight for territory, but Eldates seemed to assume there was more than enough for everyone. Depending on their numbers, we would need to take over the rest of the world to have enough space for all of us. I had no loyalty to any of the other kingdoms, but they likely wouldn't just turn over for anyone. "We will have to make it work somehow."

"You didn't hear, did you?" Izotza wiped her eyes again and sat up straighter. "Aedan wants us to go to the other worlds. We may not stay here, and we definitely won't be staying together."

"That doesn't make any sense." I glared at the moon rising lazily in the distance. "That's not how dragons work. Why would we give up our territory just because he says so?"

"He said that we can rule the roost of our own lands. Give up territory for a bigger piece somewhere else." She picked at her nails with a scowl. "Maybe I can go somewhere that isn't so hot."

"Do you want that?" The thought of losing our tiny horde to whatever this partnership was tore at something deeper in my heart. Then again, we were solitary creatures, and the only one you could count on to stay was your mate.

It took her a good minute to reply, but I didn't miss the sadness in her eyes. "I can't be the only ice dragon. Besides, if Aedan's mate is coming here, I definitely can't stay."

I felt the same way about Cenara bonding to my brother. Or worse, what if he broke her with this bond? I'd do anything to escape those hypothetical situations, with or without my territory.

CHAPTER 12 – CENARA

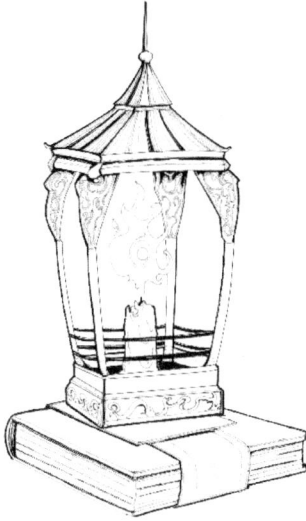

Eldates' large frame caused the cushions of the couch to tilt my body towards him. Where his skin met mine on the side of my thigh was burning hot, but it wasn't like the heat I'd experienced from even the tiniest caress from Valk.

Don't look after where he'd gone. I shouldn't even think about Valk or the way his touch made me want things that I'd not asked for in centuries. I was young and naïve then. Now, I'm strong and powerful. I'm a high priestess in a war between the gods that the universe won't know is happening until it is far too late. How did someone like him manage to ruffle my feathers so perfectly? I knew I'd never get that answer so why bother asking silly questions?

"Where were you today?" Eldates asked, brushing his lips over my shoulder. "I know Valk was talking with you before we returned, but then you were nowhere to be found. Your scent lingered in my cavern. I'm not too proud to admit that I'd hoped you were in my bed when I went to rest."

"Ah. . ." Well, that did catch me off guard. How could I reply to that without getting caught up in my lies? What had I told Valk? Would they even compare notes? It was a chance I was going to have to take. "The healer's potion makes me a bit woozy; I took a wrong turn when I left this space. Valk was quick to recover me and set me straight."

"That's right, I'd forgotten you were injured the night before." He leaned in closer, sliding his arm around me, tugging me closer. "Are you recovered now?"

"I should be by the time we do the bonding ritual." I kept my voice low and glanced around the room as if shy. Valk had vanished, and though I was loath to admit it, my heart sank.

"I see," Eldates hummed thoughtfully before using his finger to guide my face back to him. "I have a few questions about the bonding that weren't outlined in the contract. Walk with me?"

Finally. Aedan and I had purposefully left some details out so that we could assess the mental strength of the dragon king. That would play a role in the level of leash we'd use during the ritual. So far, he'd just gone along with everything that Aedan had put forth.

I followed him in an unhurried pace as he led us to the bridge. Aedan's gaze flickered to mine, taking note of where we were going. When I gave him a subtle nod, he moved off to attend to other matters.

More of our mages had come through the portals during the day, I noted as I looked around and spotted them masquerading into the volcanic wall. They looked too similar for the dragons to notice that new ones were coming every day. The tricky part was layering the magic to create a uniform scent.

"I'm guessing you wished to speak privately," I said, my tone teasing.

He turned around to offer his hand on the rickety bridge. I assumed that Valk or someone would have told him about my other form by now. I could catch myself the same as they all could, but I placed my hand in his anyway. I just needed to get him to the ritual altar, then I could drop the façade.

"Yes, don't you think we should? I'm sure you have questions that you don't want your companions overhearing." Eldates watched me carefully. I kept my eyes locked on him, no concern given to the danger of the raging lava under our feet. "I am king, as you know already, and with that comes a position of power among my people."

I fought down the chuckle. We'd already assessed the ties of loyalty to this chain of command. These dragons were only motivated by what suited them, not anything that he said. The only point we couldn't argue was that he appeared to be the most powerful after Aedan's assessment during the attacks the night prior. The only variable was Valk, who'd managed to not display his full abilities to either of us so far.

"I believe that we have clarified what I bring in terms of a dowry or trade for the expansive wealth of your kingdom." I kept my voice even, waiting for his question. I wouldn't have spoken at all except he'd fallen silent when we got to the end of the bridge.

"Yes, but would I be acknowledged within the mage ranks to be a leader in the same way?" Eldates specifically asked.

I nodded, understanding his inquiry.

"That. Well, yes. In a sense, that will be true. You will have an honorary position of power until after you meet *Him* and pledge your loyalty to our god."

"That's a requirement? Dragons keep no gods above our own power." With a growl, he stalked to the edge and looked down at the churning magma. "Aedan should know that."

You should know that Aedan is more powerful because of our god.

I offered him my sweetest smile and took his hand back into mine. "Of course, I understand that. It's just my position hinges on my relationship to our god in addition to my mastery of the magic. If you don't wish to, well, I would never force that on you. It's just that the mages may not respond to it as kindly. They will learn about your prowess in time."

"I guess that will have to do for now." Facing away from me, his voice was so low that I almost couldn't hear him. "Dragon culture requires your full submission in any bond. This isn't limited to the interactions between us. It will be within any structure that you are a part of. The mages won't have a choice if they honor you as their leader."

I narrowed my eyes but caught myself before I said something inappropriate. None of this would matter after the blood ritual, so how honest did I need to be with him anyway? Yet there was one thing I couldn't let slide without addressing. "I could speak with them if your ego demands it; however, the system isn't decided by any entity other than our god. I have been chosen by Him and while He approves of our union, I must stress that you shouldn't push too aggressively against that which you do not understand. All who have tried in the past did not walk among us for long."

"Are you threatening me?" Eldates snarled as he whipped around to meet my gaze straight on.

I don't need to. He would end you with scarcely a thought.
Instead of challenging him, I smiled sweetly. "Why would I ever
threaten you? Soon we will be a unified force to behold, but you
did ask to speak honestly."

Eldates stalked forward, and I barely withheld a flinch as he
grabbed my arm in a vice grip. Though my body was healed, the
memory of Aedan's recent rough handling coursed through me,
down to my toes. I managed to keep my expression neutral, but
my heart raced. Dragons were tough; if I was determined to go
toe-to-toe with them. . .well, that would sometimes mean pain.

"I'm not interested in games," he growled, dragging me
closer. "You aren't a dragon, so you don't understand the weight
of the burden I carry for my kind. The weight of the world!"

Everything in me wanted to scream for him to stop touching
me. He wasn't Aedan, who I would endure. Eldates was a fucking
pawn in this game and nothing more. I took a deep breath,
remembering the mission Aedan had tasked me with.

"I'm sure it is difficult to be king of such a powerful clan of
beasts. This bond is so that I can share the load of this burden
with you. Do you need me to protect your horde, or the treasure
you hide in your caves? Whatever it is, I will help you."

Eldates scoffed as he studied my face. Finally, his thumb
brushed over my lips, and his grip on my arm loosened
considerably. "If only I could trust you with my actual treasure.

Alas, that's what mates are for. Just how many other dragons do you have hiding in the worlds beyond the portals? I'm surprised they aren't higher in your ranks."

The dragons we had promised weren't dragons like the seven of them. If I had to make a guess at explaining them, they were more like the two-legged reptilian servants I'd seen here. Most of them only came up to my shoulders and had serpentine faces. Yet another little lie, but they called themselves dragon folk, so it wasn't really our misdirection entirely.

"There are forty of them," I answered smoothly while slowly taking a step back out of his space. "Your horde is much more powerful than they are, but with some training, you could perhaps bring them up to your greatness. About this treasure, perhaps you don't have to trust me entirely, but I do wish to help you. If you tell me its material and location. I could set up additional wards to ensure no one would touch it."

The beast chuckled and shook his head. "No one could touch it without my knowledge if I didn't allow it already. Like everything I claim, it is gold."

"Quite cocky, aren't you?" I purred in my best seductive tease. "Even you can't be everywhere all the time. I can take a hint, though. Once we bond, you might feel differently about the level of protection I can offer you."

His eyes heated at the tone I'd used, and I inwardly smiled. These beasts really didn't have much experience with women; it made the game all too easy. "There's a reason for that."

Before he could continue, a puff of black smoke went up as a messenger appeared beside me. The mage bowed to both of us before offering Salixa's magical tome to me. "For the coming blood bond."

"Very good. Tell her it will be done," I replied as my eyes fell to the glorious thing in my hands.

Salixa had been training me in this magic since I was old enough to hold a solid form, but I could count on my talons the number of times she'd let me hold this book without her. It was as ancient as the god who willed it into existence centuries before Salixa's birth. It was ratty looking, with pages falling out from the split binding, but it was magnificent. I was so touched that she would entrust something so powerful to me while I was on another planet; I wanted to cry.

"What did he say?" Eldates looked back and forth between us. "What is that old thing?"

"Oh, I'm so sorry. I'd not even realized we were speaking in our god's tongue. This is for our bonding ritual, so that I can get everything ready for it," I replied with mock shame at excluding him from the conversation.

Carefully, I flipped the book open. Intuitively, it turned to the page I needed. I knew that Eldates wouldn't be able to read it, so I turned it to him and tapped my finger on the words.

"That's oddly specific. How much work needs to be done to get ready?"

"Preparations are already underway. My mages can handle the little stuff." Like rounding up the serpent folk that would be sacrificed at the base of this volcano. Aedan had briefly considered sacrificing one of the seven dragons instead, but after seeing them in action last night, he'd vetoed that plan. To bind a dragon was going to take a lot of blood, but such were the costs of victory sometimes. "There is one thing I do need your help with though."

"What's that?"

"What's the most beautiful view here in your lands? Could you show me?" I slid my hand down his arm with a caress that warmed his skin to mine. When our hands met, I laced my fingers in his.

Every touch between us felt wrong, like a magnet pushing me away. But we were so close to completing this phase of the mission. I could pretend for just a few more days, couldn't I? I only hoped that he didn't feel it the way I did, or else this all would be for nothing.

CHAPTER 13 - VALK

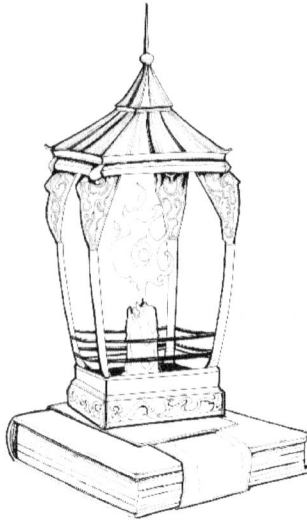

The flight across our lands hadn't done anything to calm my thoughts. The further I flew from Eldates' volcano, the angrier I got that I wasn't protecting my intended mate from whatever mysterious danger I was convinced she was in. When I turned around, I contemplated how to change Eldates' mind. Cenara wouldn't admit to having feelings for me. Without her support in my claim, it would fall on deaf ears. Nothing made sense anymore.

Aedan insisted that he couldn't bring his mate, her other lovers, and their son over until he was confident that they would be safe from those who hunted them. He claimed that this agreement and ritual were the only things that would convince them to solidify their trust in us. Were we just inviting their war to our lands? I still wasn't sure I understood the benefit of siding with a family that seemed to stir up trouble wherever they went.

On top of the fighting, why were there so many mages? I'd counted more than the original number on my flight through our lands today. Where were they all coming from? I needed a better grasp on this religion before my brother—or I—did something very stupid.

Cenara's fierce determination to save her brother and where she disappeared to all the time were other factors to consider. They were withholding something big, but I couldn't wrap my head around any of the details because I'd missed the first meetings with Eldates. Although. . .weren't we also keeping secrets? Eldates meant to subjugate Cenara and the mages to strengthen his position.

I just still couldn't shake the feeling that Eldates wasn't ready for whatever they were hiding from us. War, I could handle; I just needed to understand why. I needed a purpose before risking my life, or I'd rather trek elsewhere. The biggest problem with that plan was I knew she existed now. I wouldn't be able to walk away from her. Still, it'd be better to face this head-on and, on my terms, not the ones whispered in the shadows.

119

When I landed on the platform and shifted into my smaller form, I still hadn't quite figured out what my plan would be. How did I interact with her now? Could I wait until after she bonded with Eldates and he "gifted" her to me? My inner beast roared at that thought. If I couldn't convince her to take me instead, I wasn't sure I could avoid a battle with my brother. Ultimately, the most logical course of action was another conversation with her.

Beside the entrance where Izotza had been earlier, shadows flickered unusually against the rocky wall before Aedan stepped out and into my direct path. How had I not seen him? Was he one with the shadow? I'd seen his fire breath, so I figured he'd be a fire dragon, but now that I thought more about it, that never seemed quite right.

"Just the dragon I was looking to speak with." He crossed his arms with a cocky half-smirk plastered on his face that pissed my beast off. I wasn't as quick to anger as Sutenar, but the heat in my veins flowed all the same. "I was hoping I wouldn't have to go to your mountain to find you."

"As if that would be a difficult flight for you. Should we take this inside to include Eldates?" I tossed out in mock obedience to our new treaty. He caught my tone by the subtle shift in his eyes that spoke to the no nonsense nature I'd picked up from him. As a dragon, I didn't have much to fear in general, but there was something about him that left a tingle at the base of my spine.

"Eldates is currently occupied by Cenara with the plans for the bonding ritual. Besides, I think this needs to be between us. Dragon to dragon." Aedan took a few steps closer, studying me.

Lightning rippled off me as part of my beast pushed beneath the surface, covering my arms in scales. This display of aggression only seemed to amuse the shadow dragon.

Aedan chuckled.

"Now you see why we have to talk."

"I don't think there is anything for us to di—" I had only a fraction of a second to sidestep his charge. His fist grazed my cheek, leaving behind scorched skin even though there was no active fire. Those cautionary tingles spread from the base of my spine up my back when his body began to transform, twisting into the monster lurking under the surface. "What the fuck?"

Even as he changed, he continued to lob an assault in my direction, herding me towards the edge of the landing. Throwing my arms up to block his next strike, he pushed me back with a force that shouldn't have been possible. . .not even for a dragon.

"I don't appreciate a coward who would put our priestess in danger after offering aid and then abandon his companions when they are attacked." His words poured out in a beastly snarl, so different from the perfectly crafted sentences I'd become accustomed to. The voice vanished from the air between us and pushed into my mind as he continued to grow. *"I find you to be lazy and useless from the assessment that I have gathered during my time amongst your kind. Prove me wrong."*

The reminder that I'd been the reason she'd been hurt enraged me. Lightning ripped out of my body and cracked through the air behind me, from the sky to the trees far below. If this was a test, then I wouldn't fail. I would show him that I was more than his preconceived notions of my skill. My power wasn't shoddy, and I most certainly was not lazy, even if I'd never led a horde of dragons before. The shift tore through my body, and I barely noticed the crunch of my bones where his knuckles grazed my ribs.

"Have to make sure I'm good enough for your daughter?" I lunged in my first offensive move, just missing him, but then I spun to land a kick in his gut. Scales grew out of the pores of my skin.

"She's not my daughter, and yet she's still too much for the likes of you," Aedan snarled, catching my foot with a jaw full of teeth, twisting me straight off the edge of the cliff. Fire exploded out of the landing, and his resounding roar echoed a warning call to the danger that I was now in.

Wings tore free from my back, slowing my fall. Aedan turned his flame breath on me from the ledge above. I swerved out of the way with only a fraction of a second in my favor. Building the heat up in my throat, jolts of electricity sizzled along every inch of my scales. I flapped my wings, elevating myself to his level. The charge erupted in his direction, allowing me to catch more height.

Aedan laughed in my mind, the hint of madness toying with me. He leapt into the air and over the blast. His wings were massive, and my ego depressed, realizing he was double my size. The wind shifted based on how he sliced through the air. I followed him with only a brief thought to the recklessness, but I couldn't back down. Maybe he'd kill me, but maybe I could turn the tables in my favor.

My lightning forced the clouds to accumulate water from the environment surrounding us. If he wanted to fight, I'd give him everything I had. I had to. The only problem with dense cloud cover was that I couldn't see him. I searched the sky until a flash of light revealed his shadow to my right.

He was headed right at me!

I pivoted, narrowly avoiding his extended talons. Shadows and smoke trailed behind him. Like a rudder, that wicked tail changed his direction. I peered over my shoulder long enough to watch the shadow and smoke tie around my right foot right before he flicked me in the opposite direction. What the fuck was this beast?

A roar tore from my throat. The sky opened, dropping a heavy pelting of rain that might work. Fire illuminated his chest cavity when he turned to face me.

I summoned every bit of power I could and blasted electrified bolts from my jaws as I righted myself and circled around him. A series of explosions rocked the air currents, adding to the turbulence from our wings and the brewing storm. Four large fireballs met with the jagged trail of my power streaking about the sky. The ear-splitting cacophony left my hearing in shambles.

With a swoosh of air, my hope of taking him out plummeted. Smoke from the explosions traveled in my direction with the storm, encasing me in dense shadowy fog. I couldn't see *or* hear him! If I turned left, the wind followed, bringing the smoke with. When I dove right, the cloud continued to hover in the same place beside me.

While my power was strongest when issued directly from me, I could also target individual bolts from the summoned storm to fan out over an entire area. It might be the only shot I had left until I could ground the monster. . .

Attaching every ounce of wrath I had into the magic simmering under my scales, the world lit up.

Prismatic lightning shredded the clouds with heat as they sizzled past me in search of their target. Once free from the atmospheric prison, I ascended as fast as I could, needing a better vantage point.

Aedan's laugh danced in the back of my mind. Dark impressions ran alongside the clouds to my left as lightning continued to race across the sky. They weren't hitting him. I wasn't sure I could keep this up for much longer.

"Yes! This is exactly what I needed to ascertain from you. Eldates said that you were nothing more than a cheap copycat. Like pyrite is to gold, but this is much more impressive than I anticipated." There was marvel in his voice, though it sounded disconnected from the danger I'd put him in. He was clearly crazy.

I couldn't let what my brother had said bother me. Of course, Eldates wanted to appear to be the strongest of us all. He'd been forced to say that to seal the alliance. It also could just be lies from the mouth of a shadow serpent; I needed to keep my guard up and be prepared for anything.

"My spirit might be made of pyrite and not gold, but I'm not a cheap copy of anyone!" I roared in his mind. Aedan merely returned the comment with renewed laughter.

He dodged past me from the shadows, and I ducked to avoid a tail strike. I pivoted to the right and turned back towards the volcano before having to rear my wings back to slow my speed so I didn't crash right into Aedan. He tore through the air from below, snapping his jaw. He was impossibly fast! How?

A crimson glow signaled through the pelting rain that another attack was coming. I charged the remaining bit of lightning inside my chest cavity. I couldn't begin to guess how much I'd need to deflect this beast, but once the flame in his chest was larger than the sun in the sky, I needed to fire off my own attack and get out of the path quickly.

I discharged the lightning blasts and then twisted to the left in a harsh nosedive, allowing the torrential rain to speed my descent. None of it mattered though.

The shadow of a dragon loomed underneath me. When he smiled, his massive teeth on display, I knew I was fucked.

Aedan clamped his jaw around my throat. I roared when he flung me through the air and came crashing down the side of the cliff. Boulders and fully grown trees both broke my fall, creating a landslide as they dislodged and tumbled down the side of the volcano. With a bright flash, he shifted back into his softer form on the ledge above me. I did the same. Rain continued to fall as he stalked me. He could have killed me. In hindsight, even though I'd given it everything I had, I knew I didn't stand a chance in this fight.

"Smart dragon," he sneered. "Perhaps you do have what it takes after all."

I rose to my feet, cringing at how sore I was. He didn't offer me a hand up, didn't do anything. Just watched as I made my way up to the level where he stood. I didn't understand the backhanded compliment. I'd clearly lost.

"Despite what you or my brother think, I am more than capable. I will protect what is mine, but I still don't see a reason for me to protect what is yours." I glared at his back as he spun away to climb the rest of the way back to the landing platform. Yet another sign that he didn't feel the need to watch his back with me. Arrogant asshole.

"Don't you, though? You are entirely infatuated with something that belongs to *my* family. Cenara will bond to the king of your people. Do you understand what that means? After the blood bonding ceremony, she will only act as my son and your king demand," Aedan taunted, vanishing into the shadows as quickly as he had appeared.

I'd played my hand too casually when I'd tried to talk to Eldates, and now they both knew how to get me to fall in line. My brother could order her to be mine after he'd bonded to her, but it wouldn't be the same. I'd always know she'd chosen him as her king. I'd always know that he claimed her first and threw her away instead of cherishing her.

Rain soaked me to the bone. Aedan's words stayed with me like an anchor tethered to my wings. It wasn't a denial of what I wanted, just new terms. Unfortunately, what sat between me and the beautiful phoenix I desperately wanted for my mate. . .was my brother.

CHAPTER 14 – VALK

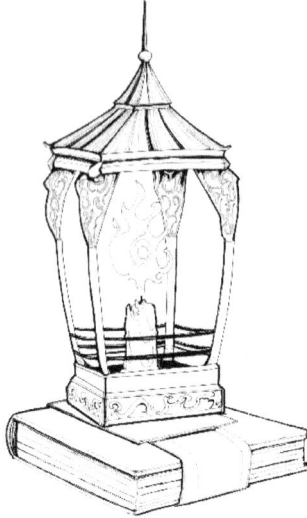

I had no idea how long I sat outside in the rain. The sky was devoid of lightning now, my power exhausted, but the continuous downpour masked my devastation at the defeat. Only Izotza would fly in these conditions, so I knew I'd be left alone; she would have gone to sleep for the night a long time ago.

The shadow dragon had called me lazy and useless. For all the frustration in my internal denial, I had to ask. . . Was he wrong? I'd spent the last few centuries running away from any sense of responsibility. I hadn't gotten involved in any of the affairs of this new world, and in turn, the other kingdoms ignored most of us, content that we stayed on our side of the planet.

Eldates was the only one who conversed with our neighbors. Nothing had inspired me; nothing had motivated me. Not until I saw her. Now something blazed in my soul, telling me I needed to do more, to *be* more. . .for her.

Cenara was driven by a sense of duty that I envied. I'd watched her attack those people without a second thought to what she was doing. No hesitation, no doubt in her heart, even as I argued with her. Instead, I became the reason she'd been hit that night. I'd put her in danger when I'd been there to help. I couldn't argue with Aedan about that. I only wish I knew what she'd told him about the spark between us. She had to feel it the way that I did, yet it didn't seem to sway her from her path.

The little phoenix would need a partner who would stand beside her. If she was my mate, surely, I could do that, couldn't I? She couldn't have known that my brother intended to discard her when it suited him or that I wouldn't even consider doing something that deplorable. I might not have been gold, but I was just as valuable. I'd protect her from her enemies. Didn't Eldates' intentions make him just that? An enemy?

I needed to speak with her, get some more insight into the way she thought about this arrangement. The sun crept up through the dissipating clouds and beyond the peaks of the mountains to the east. I sighed. She'd likely vanish again as she had done every other day so far under the sun's glow. I'd have to wait. She'd reappear at nightfall. I still had another two days before the ritual. Until then, I needed to figure out who I was going to be.

Was there a way to make my brother step aside? One that didn't mean a full-on fight with my only related beast? I shifted again, taking flight, scarcely noticing that I was moving solely out of habit. My soaked body ached from the brutal beatdown that Aedan had given me. The more I moved my wings, the more I felt the strain in each of the tendons. Even in this position, I wouldn't let my pride sulk from the loss. He'd wanted to teach me a lesson about the reality of the world that they'd come from. I could learn. For her, I would.

A constant storm raged around the mountain that I had claimed as my own. The storm, created by the blood used to mark my space, echoed my mood. It kept visitors away during the worst of my temperaments, even my "all-powerful" brother. The patter of rain matched my melancholy, and lightning flashed with no answering roar as my mind calmed.

How drastically everything had shifted in such a short span of time. My desire to please Cenara. My indecision about what to do with my current lack of standing. Aedan's words. My call to be something greater than I'd ever thought to be. And I would go toe-to-toe with the beast who'd put me in my place. One day.

Eyeing the table leaning against the wall with all my mapping utensils, I flipped it, smashing it to pieces. Shards ricocheted off the stone wall and flew in my face. I'd have to carve a new one now, but I couldn't deny how the destruction eased my tension. Dragons were obsessive, passionate, and rough. Somehow, I'd been trapped by a pair of sun-colored eyes that wouldn't pick me first. Not above her family, not above her god, not above her duty. Could I be second to all of that? Yes. But I couldn't be second to *him*. Eldates would have to stand aside. He'd have to let me have her and work out a new deal if he wanted to stay king. That was the only way forward.

Velenu cleared his throat. An involuntary snarl tore from my chest as I whipped around to face him.

He tucked a strand of longer hair behind his ear with a nervous expression. The simple act of refusing to meet my gaze displayed his unwillingness to fight me, soothing the need to defend my territory in seconds. "I'd been calling for you since before you entered, but you didn't hear me."

"Sorry," I apologized, and in this instance, I meant it. It wasn't his fault I was in this position with Aedan, Cenara, and my brother. "I've got a lot of things going on. What do you need?"

At my invitation, he shuffled forward into the main cavern of my lair, leaving a few feet between us. "I have to say that after the past few days, I'm even more nervous about this agreement.

I'm concerned about Eldates. Shadows move strangely now, even during the day! Yet he seems to ignore the changes happening in our environment."

I let out an exhausted sigh as I considered his words. I didn't think the influx of mages was anything to be all that concerned with, but maybe there were additional issues to address. "What do you want me to do about it?"

"Shadows aren't meant to creep around in the day." He emphasized the point again before swallowing hard and leaning closer. "I can't help but feel as if we are allowing evil to seep into our grounds."

"Evil? Really, Velenu?" I didn't bother to cover my chuckle. I'd not been paying too much attention to the mages since that first night, clearly absorbed in whatever Cenara was up to. I'd not seen the mages that were assigned to me; they had to be down in the depths of my territory, even if they were soaking wet all the time. Or they'd found other accommodations.

"Don't mock me. I think you might be the only one who can help Eldates see reason," he pleaded. "I know Aedan is powerful, but you and Eldates together. . .it might be the only chance that we have. I don't want to bond to these mages, even if they are here to enhance my abilities."

He had no idea how powerful the shadow dragon was. Or maybe he'd watched the fight. His train of thought had merit, though. With Aedan out of the way, all the issues of our current situation would fade away. I could pursue and claim Cenara as my mate without having to be king of this horde. Aedan was the problem in that plan, and I liked the idea of removing him a whole lot more than harming Eldates. Even though my bones and bruises healed rapidly while I spoke with my companion, I'd not missed the point of my thorough beating. I was the weaker dragon.

However, with Eldates—and maybe Lawry or Sutenar—we could take him down.

I wouldn't give Velenu hope that I was considering his commentary just yet. "Have you vocalized this concern to my brother?"

A deep frown pulled at the corners of Velenu's lips, and he shook his head. "I waited around all night yesterday for a moment to talk with him. He even looked at me a few times, but he was having a pretty serious talk with that high priestess. They talked for hours, mages coming in and out of the conversation. I finally gave up and decided to talk to you first."

The reminder about Cenara being with Eldates the evening prior did not help settle the rage in my gut, but it did help sway me further towards removing Aedan. And yet my hands were tied. Persuading Lawry to fight with me for this cause was a sure thing, but convincing Eldates would be tricky. If there were other dragons out there, he wouldn't just give them up for the sake of maintaining the order we had here. He'd been meeting with the mages for weeks before we were introduced. Who knew what Eldates' end goal was? One thing at a time. I needed to talk to her before I finalized any plans.

"What did you want in your life? Before all of this. . .nonsense," I asked while pondering the deeper questions I'd been asking myself.

Who did I want to be in my life? What did I truly want? I'd given in to contentment and comfort, for what?

There were times when I questioned if Velenu was really a dragon with his lack of fury in our interactions. He had never been one to make hasty statements, so I waited patiently while he considered my question before replying.

"Well, I just wanted to spend time with my books. I wanted to be the smartest dragon alive."

"Even though you would have no one to share that knowledge with?" I raised my eyebrow.

Dragon mates were chosen, but we as a species often decided being alone was easier. I wondered if, on some level, that wasn't just more complacency.

"I might travel one day," Velenu said softly with a shrug.

Velenu, travel? I gave him a dubious look, and he laughed.

"We live a mighty long time. I could eventually wish to travel. But if doing so meant I couldn't read any more books. . .well, I guess one must always have a consequence for enjoying what you love. What about you? You spent so much time flying the clouds, we wondered if you would ever come down."

That was all I wanted to do. Fly. To what end? For what purpose? I couldn't say outside of exploring more of the world to put down on my maps. We could soar higher than most other creatures that we'd encountered so my maps could give others a glimpse of what they were missing.

"I wanted to find excitement, to breathe life back in me. It is dull here."

"You should read more then," he chastised with a smirk tugging his cheeks.

"Reading will not settle the lightning in my blood. It's finally moving for the first time in many centuries. . ." How could I begin to explain the way Cenara made me feel when I saw her in— either of her forms? The way she flew, like a blazing inferno or a shooting star. How her lips felt pressed to mine as I fought every urge to pull her closer and explore her for hours. Even the simple joy of knowing I could fly with her.

"Then you aren't reading the right books," Velenu retorted.

It was my turn to chuckle. I'd never win this conversation. "Look. About the shadows. I'll keep my eye on the mages a little more closely, but if Eldates isn't concerned, shouldn't we trust him? He knows them all a lot better than we do; maybe there's something that is missing from our understanding."

"Yes. His individual thought process is missing." Velenu straightened his shirt, his face pinched in frustration. "He should have had the first meeting with just us as a horde. But now, I'd trust it more if you and Eldates were in agreement. I want to hear from Eldates. Not from him and Aedan."

I clapped him on the shoulder and caught his eyes. "Let me see what I can learn about the situation. If I say it's okay, then you'd follow me?"

He looked thoughtful for a moment before replying. "Yes."

With that vote of confidence, I'd weigh out the decision in front of me. But first, I needed to talk to my little bird to know which fight was looming in my future.

CHAPTER 15 - CENARA

Another day lost. The golden hues of light that condemned me to live on the edge of nonexistence slipped behind the clouds. I wanted to weep. My wings missed the warmth of the sun, the gliding winds. Honestly, I didn't know why I missed it so much. Nothing had changed in centuries, and from the way Keane spoke about our mission, it would be many more centuries to go. Someday, things would be different.

The main cavern of the volcano was fairly quiet. Only Izotza and one of the poison dragons lingered in the commonplace. Attempts to make short conversation with either of them was moot; they'd be drones by tomorrow. Tomorrow night, I'd be blood bound to their stupid king and this whole charade would erupt into ashes. I'd be tied to Eldates, but I would do what I must for the sake of our mission.

I felt the scorch of his gaze before seeing him walk in from the landing. Did he time my return to their plane?

Valk. Handsome, torturous Valk. With his heated stare urging me to push the boundaries of what I shouldn't dare to want. I could lie to the others but not to myself. I wanted what he teased me with. I wanted his mouth against my skin and him buried inside. He tormented my restless soul during the days when I could do nothing but live amongst my thoughts. None of these beautiful visions could come to pass, but it didn't mean a woman couldn't dream.

When he hadn't returned last night, I'd cursed myself for somehow messing up before I'd been able to even attempt a game between the two dragons. I couldn't take back what I'd said to Valk the night prior. I needed to keep Eldates' attention fixed on me, keep him blind. With a little more than luck, he wouldn't see the shadows taking over his lands or notice the influx of mages silencing his waitstaff, depleting their resources.

Today, Aedan asked Eldates to join him while they scouted locations for our new family "home," claiming he needed the dragon's insight.

Eldates' dragon ate up the lie, savoring the stroke to his ego like it was the most decadent dessert he'd ever tasted. Men. It didn't matter what species they were. Vanity reigned supreme, and as long as we needed his compliance, we could pretend to be dependent on him. Tomorrow, it would all end. I could be patient.

I glanced over my shoulder to Valk, and as our eyes met, I cast them down in that submissive way he seemed to like. Taking a deep breath, I settled my racing heart. This was the only difference between the brothers. Valk excited me. He shouldn't have been on the radar at all, but here he was, shifting even Aedan's plans in a dangerous game that I wasn't sure any of us would win. In the end, though, it only mattered if my brother won.

A hand caressed my hip as an imposing brick of man pressed into my back. He moved so quickly that I didn't notice him in the flurry of my thoughts. His hot breath glided over my neck, sending a chill down my spine.

"I thought we talked about you doing that, my fiery mate." His husky voice chastised me in a way that promised a delicious sort of punishment for pushing his buttons.

"And I believe we talked about *that*. . ." I attempted to step away; I couldn't let him have control of our interactions. This was my game, and we were going to play it my way. Yet something about him always threw me off. He was so focused on me, my every expression, each body movement I made, each thing that piqued my interest. Eldates was only interested in the power promised to him from this bonding. Not that I didn't understand where he was coming from; power from our union was all I was after too.

His nose trailed over my skin. Pinning me against him, he inhaled deeply. He didn't even care that the other two dragons were watching. "Have you ever been worshipped by your past lovers, Cenara?"

Warmth surged through my body, his words repeating in my mind. I fought to keep my head from falling back, from giving into the desire he ignited deep within. Hell, I couldn't even remember my own name, let alone the last man who'd touched me. "What kind of question is that?"

Did the words even come out? I'd almost caught my breath when he continued, his voice dropped lower while his lips moved down my shoulder.

"If you haven't, then they were all fools. You may be a high priestess, but I am going to show you how devout a dragon is when they find their treasure."

Did he just call me a treasure? That couldn't be right.

"Valk. . .please don't do this," I begged him, trying to prolong the game. It was the only reply I could think of but saying Valk's name proved to be too much. He spun me in his arms and tossed me over his shoulder.

"Hey!" I glanced around to see if anyone would stop whatever this was, but Aedan—*when did he come in?*—only watched with an amused smirk. *Screw him and his stupid plans.*

The other two dragons looked anywhere but in our direction, a hint of embarrassment coloring their cheeks. I pounded my fists on Valk's back before I tried to shift.

Valk's growl rumbled against the tops of my thighs pressed against his chest. I felt a quick swat on my ass. . .snapping me out of my shift! In the burgeoning night sky, he walked out onto the platform. Without a second thought or a moment to discuss how he was out of his goddamn mind; he leapt off the edge. Wind blazed past us in our rapid descent, and the world below came rushing to greet us. He tossed me forward into a free fall. I willed my wings to manifest, but he was faster, shifting with a roar and catching me in one of his claws.

"Valk! Stop this!" I shouted, using my hands to try and pry his talons open. "You and I have different definitions of worship if you think that this is okay!"

"Just be patient," he promised, speaking through my mind. I shivered again, but it had nothing to do with the chilled air of this evening flight.

141

"I will not! You will turn around right this instant or release me!" My voice hardly carried over the wind, but he glanced back, so I knew he heard something. If I could get him to drop me, I could shift and get away. I hated being carried in this vulnerable position. The more I struggled, the tighter his grip became, and I only hurt my hands trying to work against his scales.

Open forests, pristine waters, a world unblemished by pollution and warfare went whizzing by below us. This was how most of the planets had looked before my family arrived. When I'd been young, I used to think the scenery was beautiful. It wasn't until Salixa had informed me how much this sort of environment hurt my brother that I'd begun to shun the softness. Planet after planet, we'd optimized the terraforming to transition from this to shadows and chaos in only a handful of years, depending on the resources available to us. Here, the dragons would help expedite that process.

Lightning rumbled in the sky further ahead on the path he was taking. I tossed a glance up to the black dragon holding me. "You are flying us straight into a storm!"

"*Yes, I know.*" Valk's tone held a note of amusement aimed at my obvious dismay. Why was he messing with me like this?

"You know that I am going to fly away as soon as you set me down, right?" I informed him with a hint of frustration in my voice. It wasn't the first time a man had tried to capture me; I just thought Valk was smarter than that. I clearly didn't know him very well.

He didn't reply with words. A soft but thundering purr came from his massive chest, almost as if he was trying to soothe me. Begrudgingly, it almost worked. . .until we became drenched from the storm he'd flown us straight into. I resumed my pounding on the top of his talon to get him to drop me.

Lightning flashed all around Valk. A bolt raced right by my dangling feet. I tucked my body into as small of a ball as I could, feeling truly afraid for the first time. Fire and wind I could handle; in this form, I could even deal with the rain. But lightning? I don't think there is a bird alive that is enthusiastic about lightning.

For how big of a moving target he was, Valk didn't seem the least bit concerned. He glided between the lightning bolts with grace and ease as if this were nothing more than a gentle spring breeze. The clouds cleared and rocks rushed towards us from the side of another mountain. Before I could shout a warning, he twisted, catching a current and then landed on a ledge.

He shook the rain from his wings and body in the dark tunnel. I covered my face to block from the droplets but found myself wrapped in his smaller form's arms only a moment later, shivering as the water dripped down every inch of my body. Despite shaking off, Valk was still soaking wet. The deep purr rumbled against me. I hated to admit it, but it calmed me,

143

allowing me to breathe a sigh of relief while taking in our new surroundings.

For all my bravado about flying away once he set me down, the storm outside had me rethinking that strategy. On one hand, I couldn't work with Eldates if I wasn't back at the volcano with the others. But. . .where exactly was I?

The storm raged on, lightning flashing enough to show there were three more exits. He'd not planned this capture very well. As soon as the storm subsided, it wouldn't be hard for me to get out.

"Where are we?" I finally asked, breaking the silent tension. Compared to the volcano, this mountain cavern was devoid of embellishments. Further in, a large canvas was attached to the wall, but I couldn't make out many other details.

He paused to gather a towel from grooves in the cavern wall. "This is my home."

Oh no. This was not where I needed to be right now. I shoved against him with both of my hands and wiggled to get down onto my feet. Valk caught my wrist before I could get too far away and pulled me in closer to him. While I struggled against his muscular grip, his eyes met mine.

"Stop. We need to talk. I can't be overheard. I don't think the others will particularly like what I have to say."

My heart sped up in my chest. Just what had he figured out? I knew Aedan had taken him out for a discussion while I was with Eldates, but I also knew that our plan remained unchanged. This could be problematic. "So, you steal me from the volcano hall? You could have just asked for a conversation like your brother did."

His eyebrow twitched as he took a deep breath to calm himself. "I am trying my best to be rational, but little bird, you are pushing every single button of mine. I have made it clear to nearly everyone that my desire is to claim you as my mate. Yet it seems like the situation is forcing a turn of events that I don't know if I am able to abide by. I need to hear what you want out of this situation. Not Aedan, not Eldates. You."

Well, he sure didn't hold back any of the dialogue. I could tell Valk was more perceptive than some of the other dragons from how he'd watched me before. I wasn't sure just how much he knew, and I wasn't willing to show my hand first. I couldn't meet his gaze as I figured out where to start. Would I find fury or heat in his expression? I wasn't sure which I would have preferred. An involuntary shiver tore down my body, my lip trembling from the cold water slowly sinking into my pores.

"Dammit. This is not a great start to the conversation. I'm a terrible mate. You are freezing. I know just the thing." Valk pulled me against him, cradling my body with one hand and using the towel to pat me dry with the other. He then lifted me, taking us down a side tunnel that descended at a steep angle.

With each step, the temperature rose. The dark passage was illuminated only by glowing mushrooms framing the path. I wanted to protest, to beat his chest and scream at him that I could walk. But between his body's heat and the purring. . .I was too comfortable.

A new cavern opened up to us. In the center were seven large craters filled with steaming water billowing into the room. Valk set me down gently next to one of the pools, making sure my feet were stable before releasing me. I grabbed the towel to wrap around me, but he yanked it from my hands.

"Take off your dress," he demanded, walking over to another hole in the wall lined with linens.

My mouth fell open, and I shook my head at his back. "I will not. You don't get to force me into your home, drop me in your private hot springs, and then demand I strip for you."

Valk's eyes heated when he closed the space between us. I wrapped my hands around my waist, shivering again, but I kept my expression firm. Even while gazing at his chiseled chest and not his face. One of his hands settled on the curve of my hip, the other tangled in my hair. Tugging my head back so that I was looking into his eyes, he dipped me back. I was entirely at his mercy.

"You will take off your cold, wet dress, or I will do it for you with my teeth before I bury my face in between those legs of yours."

Valk grazed his lips over mine as if to emphasize his point. Though he fully supported my weight, I trembled again. I pressed my mouth to his, unable to stop myself. I wrapped an arm around his neck to pull him closer, deeper. I'd been handled roughly almost all my life, but for some reason, his heavy-handed grip was gentle. Safe. Secure. His threats were only meant to turn me on. . .and my body was singing for him.

Lightning, sparks, flashes—whatever the fuck they were— grew between us with each brush of his tongue against mine. Each caressing tease enhanced the flame in my gut that made my soul fly even while my wings were hidden. In that moment, I made a decision. One that Aedan might not approve of, but fuck it. . . He let me get stolen away.

"I want you to," I whispered against his temple when he pulled his lips from mine to press kisses down my neck.

"As you wish." Valk's voice turned husky, and his grip cupped my ass to hold me in place. As if I would go anywhere else. He'd been torturing me for days, maybe without that intent, but I needed him to make good on his promises.

Kisses led to soft bites along my skin while he pulled the dress down off my shoulders. His teeth nibbled the sensitive spot on my clavicle as he popped the first button. Valk was unhurried, sampling each part of the new flesh he exposed, but I needed him to move faster. After tomorrow, he'd be a drone, and I'd be bound to his brother. I could only have this tonight, and I wanted all of it.

I felt every button as they popped open. He kissed his way down between my heavy breasts. His fingers seared through the fabric on my thighs. The slow, torturous pace drove me crazy; I wanted him to take me faster.

Pop. Kiss. *Pop.* Kiss.

I ran my hands through his hair before realizing the dress was only being held by the sleeves that clung to my elbows. Still, he moved lower and lower, sinking down to his knees, caressing my skin with his lips just above the line of my panties. He stopped, tormenting me by trailing his nose along the thin fabric.

Valk growled deeply when I pulled away to toss the dress off my arms. It pooled in a heavy, wet mass on the floor by my feet. His fingers dug into my ass as he used his teeth to pull the offending lace out of his way. His tongue slowly licked from my belly button down to my clit.

I met his hungry gaze when he set me on a smooth stone by the boiling water. The warmth erased the lingering chill from my skin, adding to the growing desire building within. A whimper escaped from me when he pulled away, his eyes dancing over my body.

"I keep telling myself that I'm not entirely enraptured by you, that I still hold a shred of the dragon I was before." Valk spoke softly, his fingers caressing from the swell of my breast to the top of my knee. "But I'd be insane to not have become so ensnared."

Using his left knee to slide my legs apart, he lowered his head, placing one, two, three kisses on the top of my stomach. His hands slid under my legs and tilted my body towards him, the heat of his breath hitting all my sensitivities. With one final inhale, Valk descended on me, and a moan tumbled from my lips.

His tongue stroked and twirled as he discovered how my body responded to his exploration. He wrapped his lips around my clit, teasing me with gentle bites, sucks, and licks. I tossed my head back, my toes curling. The sound of his satisfied groan was a treasure I'd keep to myself for all the years to come.

"Valk. . ." I encouraged as my body tightened with his leisurely pace.

Mine.

Was that his thought or mine? Normally, our kinds couldn't communicate in our minds unless one of us had shifted, but I didn't have another moment to think about it as he dragged his fingers through my soaking need. I cried out when he pushed them deep inside of me and sucked on my clit hard. I came undone, my head lifting from the warm stone as I tried, and failed, to contain my ecstasy.

Valk worked his tongue and his fingers through my orgasm, extending the waves rolling through my being. He didn't leave an inch of my flesh undiscovered. Each touch full of passion, heat and, dare I say, worship?

I came again, faster than I ever had in my life.

"More, please. . ." I begged. If I only got one night, I wanted all of it.

Valk chuckled against my hip before kissing me there. "I'm thinking the exact same thing, little bird."

He crawled over my body and claimed my mouth. The taste of my desire all over his lips as he dominated each exchange of our tongues left me breathless. He lowered his pelvis to mine. At first, I was annoyed that he was still wearing clothes, but then I realized the heavy weight pressing against my thigh. . .wasn't his leg.

Valk took my right hand and pulled it between us, wrapping it around his girth as he thrusted, still clothed, through my grip. He growled against my mouth when I slid down to repeat the motion. He was *huge*. I wasn't sure exactly how this was going to work. I was beginning to understand why he was taking his time, but my body decided she didn't like that game.

With a mere flick of my fingers, the linen between us lit to flames. Valk chuckled darkly. I tightened my grip as his flesh met my palms. I twisted my way up his length until I could squeeze the precum from his head onto my thumb.

"Impatient, are we?" He nipped at my lips and lowered his body to slide against mine, the flames moving around to his sides and back. "I just want to make sure you understand what it means for me to be inside of you."

"Enough delays. Valk, I need you to fuck me," I growled, moving my body up to catch his tip to my entrance. "If I break, well, that's my problem later."

"Lover, settle into my pace," he crooned back as he pushed into me, but just the tip of that monster. He scooped under my shoulder to flip us so that he was sitting with his feet in the water, and I was sitting on top of him. His grip controlled my descent as I gasped against his shoulder while he split my body in half. "You are so tight, Cenara. Relax, little one. I know you can take me."

Inch by inch, he thrust up to adjust my body to the all-encompassing feeling. His dick radiated heat and lightning teased my sensitive places, sending jolts of pleasure through me from head to toe. I clung to him, my nails digging into his skin until I heard him curse under his breath as my ass met his thighs.

Mine.

We locked eyes for one crucial moment, releasing any worry that this wouldn't be possible. I wrapped my arms around his neck and pressed the rest of my body against him. My lips met his again in an inflamed need.

I rose just enough for me to slam him all the way back in and then everything else was lost to the crashing carnal desire as he hit me in all the right places until I shattered again and again. When I wasn't sure if I could survive another orgasm, Valk's roar shook the entire cavern. His claws, holding me so tightly, sliced my thighs, marking what was now his.

How was I supposed to walk away from the dragon now?

CHAPTER 16 - VALK

Cenara lay with her back pressed against my chest, half asleep thanks to all the orgasms. I'd carried her back up the tunnel to the warming stone in my nest. As a dragon, I often slept right on the stone and always alone. But an insipid rock wasn't the best for sharing a nest with a woman. She seemed to sense my hesitation, and with a few whispered words, shadows manifested in the nest to cushion rounds two and three.

I'd been concerned that I would hurt her, but she'd only asked for more after checking on the status of the storm beyond the tunnels. If she was waiting for the storm to end, she'd be in my bed for the rest of our lives, because I'd never let it cease.

My lover shifted to rest her face into the crook of my neck. For how many centuries it had been for me, I was grateful for my stamina. I would gladly bury myself in her again, but she'd finally begun to doze.

"My fiery little mate," I crooned and dropped a kiss on her temple. "Let's talk about what comes next." So preoccupied with each other's bodies, we had avoided the conversations that needed to happen before the forthcoming ritual.

She didn't move her head, her voice heavy with sleep. "What do you mean?"

"You are mine. Surely, you must know that like I do." I pressed on the heart of the matter. "I want to claim you. Instead of just a blood bond, we could add the mating dance."

"This can't be more than what it is this evening, Valk," she said, still content in my arms. "I must bond to the dragon king."

"You would still try to flee this, knowing that his touch wouldn't be like mine?" To emphasize my point, I caressed my hand up the side of her leg, and she shifted against me with a small, needy pant.

"My life isn't about what I want. I. . ." She hesitated and then shook her head. "You'd never understand."

That was the crack I needed to get into the true purpose of all of this. There was so much in that tiny admission, and now was my only window to go for it.

"Give me a chance to understand," I whispered, kissing her shoulder.

"You aren't going to believe me, but here goes." Cenara took a deep breath and lifted her head to see me. I kept my face neutral and focused on listening to whatever she was about to tell me. "My brother is a god, but he's lost a lot of his strength. I met him after the other gods had stripped him of his power."

"Is this brother actually Aedan's son?" I asked for clarification. The mighty dragon had insisted that Cenara wasn't his daughter, but that was something to address later. Her brother being the god that she was devoted to, that all the mages were devoted to, made sense to me for some weird reason.

For a moment, Cenara hesitated as if she wasn't going to continue. "Yes. He's Salixa's only birthed child. Some of her other mates don't mind when I call them father, but Aedan doesn't like it when I use it."

"And there is nothing romantic between you and this god?" Her devotion to this being gave me the first rise of worry. I knew she responded better to me than my brother, but if I were competing against a god? How could I even hope to stand a chance?

Cenara crinkled her beautiful nose and shook her head. "Not like that, but he's been everything to me in my life. Early on, I was the only external source of faith in him when they cast him out of the heavens, and he was my protector." Her eyes shone a little differently as she swam through memories. "My phoenix father tried to kill him before I hatched, or so they told me. Salixa was my first imprint when I entered my life, and she brought me to sit before her son. My eggshell was still attached in most places." A small chuckle escaped from her, and she settled back in closer to me.

I could hardly breathe, not wanting to disturb her from the peace that captivated her. Her hands absently trailed from my thighs to my knees and back up again. My dragon craved every touch, and I couldn't stop the soft purr that tumbled out. It didn't seem to distract her, and for that, I was thankful. I needed answers before figuring out my next move.

"I almost think that his parents had expected something different to happen from the shock on their faces. But he'd taken one look at me and said to Salixa, 'She's like me.' After that, we were inseparable until I was older and realized he needed my help."

I struggled with how to ask the next question, but in the end, I figured it was better to be direct. "In what way were you like him? Is he a phoenix too?"

"No, like I said, he's a god, but. . .how do I say this?" She tossed a glance back at the rain outside over our shoulders and frowned. "I guess you are about to find out anyway. If I can't get out of here before daybreak, all will be revealed. I really thought the storm would have passed by now."

I remained quiet even though I could disperse the storm. Cenara always appeared on edge and demure before, but here the tension dissolved. I'd keep her trapped here forever if I could get away with it, but at some point, Aedan would come looking for her.

"I'm not just a phoenix. When I was a child, I could switch between all my forms as I wished. There are the two that you have seen and. . .another."

"You don't have to hide from me. I truly want to know you, Cenara." I wrapped her up tightly in my arms and though she tried to hide it, I noticed the hint of a smile cross her lips.

"My mother was a fire esper. She was one with the element and lived within the flames of the gods—the fire that burned for centuries. But you see, the trouble with espers is that without the flame to keep us burning, we flicker out."

An esper? I'd never even heard of such a creature. "You moved between the three forms when you were a child, but what about now?"

Her eyes dropped to her hands as she ran them along the tops of my arms. "As I approached maturity, my brother's power began to wane as resources were depleted. We had to flee to a new planet to secure more mages; a god's power is dependent on

157

the acolytes' faith and abilities. My esper side couldn't withstand the harsh winds on our new home and she withered. Only Aedan's flame helps me survive through the day until the winds settled in the evening. I think that's part of the reason he resents me; I'm unable to aid my brother when I am in that state. But we haven't found a way to reverse what happened. Only when my brother's power is restored, can I hope to have the full scope of my life back."

I couldn't kill Aedan then, not unless *I* became the source of her survival. How could I when the heat in my blood became lightning, not fire? This conversation was doing exactly what I'd hoped it would: give me options. The only problem was that the options presented weren't ideal.

"I just remembered something," she said, sitting up on her knees in front of me, distracting me from my thoughts to give her my full attention. "You said I could see your treasure if I came to your cavern. But I understand if you've changed your mind."

There was an excited glint in her eyes while she waited patiently for my response. I cupped her cheeks in my hands and guided her face forward until our foreheads touched. "I did say that, didn't I?"

"Yes, and your cavern is so bare that I can't imagine where you would possibly hide such a treasure." Cenara laughed, closing her eyes, and brushing her nose along mine. The joy she exuded from something as simple as being here with me gave me a rush that I'd not experienced in a long time.

I partially shifted to expose the scales along my chest. Her beautiful eyes snapped open. I removed my hand from her waist and slid the scales aside to show her the one buried underneath.

"It's gold?" Her hand hovered above the scale; her eyes were mesmerized by the sight of it.

"Pyrite. My brother's obsession is gold."

"Can I touch it?" she asked, hesitant. When I nodded, she grazed the surface with the tips of her fingers. "It's attached to you?"

"It's removable, but I'll only give it to my mate," I teased as the slow purring began again in my chest. "It comes with special powers that make me unable to deny the holder anything. Not unlike what I'm willing to do for you already. Cenara, I would give you the world if you asked for it. With you as my mate, I wouldn't feel the need to protect this scale from you."

She glanced between it and me while processing my words. There was a hint of a blush on her cheeks. "Are all your treasures actually scales? For every dragon?"

I still hadn't figured out why she was so interested in these particular treasures, but I replied with a shrug. "Pretty much."

"And you will only give it to your mate?" she clarified, resting her hand on my shoulder.

159

"That's correct." She didn't seem to understand that all she had to say was that she would allow my claim, and I'd give it to her if it meant that much.

Cenara leaned forward, pressing her body against mine. I grew hard again as she kissed her way up my chest to my waiting mouth. "After I'm forced to bond to your brother, can I see you again before your blood ritual?"

I hated her use of the word 'forced,' but I didn't miss the true nature of her question. She wanted me, and if given the choice, she would pick me.

"That's not how it works with dragons, Cenara. I will not be your lover in the shadows while he puts his hands on you. I want you as mine and mine alone. If you tell me now that this is what you want too, then I will insist that I am the one you are bonded to." None of what I said had been untruthful, but I didn't want it to come down to a fight between my brother and me. "Just agree to be mine, and we can sort out the rest of it."

"I can't. The terms are very specific." She rose up to straddle me, holding the blanket around her to shield herself from the frigid storm air whistling through the cavern. "I'll have to think of something else then. I'm not going to be able to forget about you for quite a while after the ritual. What magic have you used on me?"

I leaned forward and kissed her with a smile growing on my lips. Her question was just a tease, but I would answer anyway. "There's no magic to this. You must be sensing my obsession, my pure will to please, protect, and cherish you. I really owe Lawry an apology. I think I finally get why he won't let Izo get too far away. You have bred a madness in me that must feel like magic to you."

The truth of my brother's intentions weighed heavily on me, but if it would offer her respite, maybe I could deal with it until he discarded her. This way, she wasn't hurt, and she saw it coming.

"I need to tell you about Eldates' plan," I started and immediately felt the crashing guilt of betraying my brother.

"Do we have to talk about him?" She kissed the sensitive skin under my ear and pressed her breasts against my chest.

"It might be the workaround that you would prefer." Cenara froze against me, and I knew I had her attention. "He doesn't intend to mate you. He wants to take a dragon from the ones you are bringing. I hate having to say this next part, but he says once he's done with you, you could be ours. When he releases you, I can make the claim, and the others won't be able to touch you. That way, you do what your family wants but then you still come back to me. I don't want to do it this way. . .but I just thought you should know."

A light, amused laugh escaped from Cenara. "I won't wait for him to be 'done with me' before I am back in your nest if that's his intention. I'll give him a sleeping tonic and fuck you in his bed. Once the rituals are done, none of it will matter anyway. Besides, if this storm doesn't end soon, I may not have much longer if I can't get back to Aedan's flame. This will all be so short-lived. But what a way to go in the end."

Her body moved so that my hard cock slid through her wetness. Despite her insistence that she had to bond to Eldates, it seemed she couldn't stay off me any more than I could keep my hands off her. Even when I held her roughly, she submitted, understanding my intent was to give her nothing but pleasure. She'd spoken almost as crudely as Eldates had, but in this instance, I liked what she was promising me. Her soft skin trembled under my caresses as she settled me fully inside of her.

"Use my fire instead of Aedan's," I murmured. Did I fully comprehend what I was offering? No. But whatever he gave her had to be something that I could do too. And I vowed I wouldn't be second to any other in her life.

Cenara gasped when I thrust, her nails cutting into the soft skin devoid of scales. Breathless, she panted, "I have to admit I'm a bit scared about this plan. . .what if it doesn't work?"

Her confession of vulnerability gave me the opportunity to step up and show her that I could be what she needed.

"You will not fade out in my care. I will give you all of myself. Do whatever you need to do to survive, knowing that I will keep you safe," I demanded before kissing her roughly.

She hesitated only briefly before she complied. A sharp stab of pain sliced through my gut.

Cenara pulled strands of flame from my core fire. It burned like nothing else I'd ever experienced in my life. A hot glow illuminated both of us. My beast snarled, not wanting to appear weak in front of our mate. I rolled her over, making sure I stayed deep inside her tight body. With the blanket cushioning her from the smooth, unforgiving rock, I pinned her down, growling through the growing pain. I pounded into her. The little phoenix took the pace in stride with encouraging shouts of my name as her flame latched onto mine.

Her orgasm dragged me into my own, and I emptied everything I had inside of her. When I pulled out, she stroked the back of her hand down my cheek, drawing my attention to her again. She studied me, a ghost of a smile crossing her lips.

"It might be stupid, but. . .I trust you."

Little glowing orbs of red, orange, and yellow light danced around her before she faded, leaving only a fiery haze behind.

I couldn't sense her anymore beyond the painful tug on the fire in my soul telling me that she was still with me. Was this how she was forever destined to spend the daylight hours? My heart hurt for the beautiful woman who'd been born to embrace the sun.

The pain didn't matter. Cenara trusted me, and I would protect my mate at all costs. I would be whatever she needed me to be.

CHAPTER 17 – CENARA

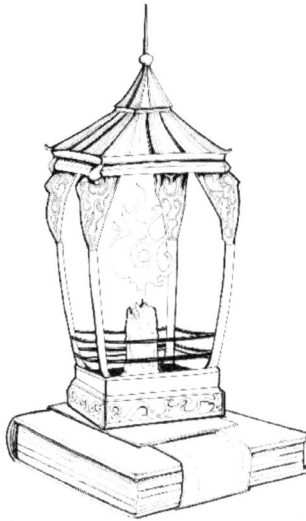

Valk managed to maintain my esper spirit throughout the day. The fire in his core was strong, stronger than I had anticipated. When I'd finally manifested as the sun set on this planet, he'd crumpled in relief from the pain he'd been burdened with. My arms had wrapped around his waist as if able to support the weight of this beast of a man.

"You are radiant as usual but are you feeling all right?" he asked cautiously, dropping the writing instrument he'd been using to work on a large canvas pinned up against the cavern wall.

"I am perfectly well." I planted a kiss on his arm as I moved around his body to see what he'd been up to. Taking in the details on the sheet in front of me, my jaw fell open. "Is this village from the other night?"

"Yeah," he admitted with a shyness I found endearing. Stupid dragon continued to grow on me. "I enjoy creating maps of the world as we see it from the sky."

A hot blush crept up my neck when I saw the extremely detailed phoenix flying through the center.

"Is that supposed to be me?"

"It is you. I'm surprised I remembered much of the world behind you and your flames. I couldn't take my eyes off you. But I'm sorry. I'll never put you in danger like that again. I just wasn't expecting your actions. To know you were struck because of me. . ." He closed his eyes, his brows furrowing with remorse.

"Valk, it's fine. I'm okay now. My esper destroys all the toxins in the transformation." I placed his hand against where the arrow had been. "You know that I am unharmed."

"Never again," Valk growled in that deliciously obsessive way he did, and I wanted to sigh. "From now on, if they are your enemies, then they are mine. If they challenge your family, they challenge me."

"That's a big promise to make. I told you that my brother intends to take on the gods. You may want to think about it."

166

I could lie to myself and say that these were just words between us. I could say that this was all going according to plan, but the script had long been thrown out. Aedan was convinced that we had to force the dragons to comply like we did with so many of our mages, yet here was Valk offering me his devotion in exchange for love. Love that I wanted to give him, especially when he looked at me that way. Did I really have to turn him into a drone if he'd do what we asked?

"I don't need to think about it anymore. You tell me what you need, and I will be at your side, no matter the consequences."

I need you to be the king. I cursed myself that I even thought the words. After meeting Eldates, I knew he would never willingly hand it over to his brother. He'd have to be forced to do so. A new plan wove in place, but I needed to be alone to make it work. "That lights something in my heart that I didn't expect."

I pulled him in for another kiss, and he scooped me up easily, pressing me against his chest. While he walked us back to his nest, I laughed against his lips. "If this rain doesn't stop soon, we are going to have to go to the rituals soaking wet."

"It's a feature of my powers; the storm will never stop around my mountain unless I will it to." Valk laid me in his soft bedding and took in my expression before he had the good sense to look ashamed for not mentioning that fact sooner. "There's still a lot we must learn about one another."

"Clearly," I mused, fighting against my irritation at his new disclosure.

"Aw, little bird, don't be angry with me," Valk cooed, caressing his hands down my new dress. "You were so peaceful last night. When was the last time someone took care of you like I want to?"

I pursed my lips and thought about it for a moment. His mouth teased soft kisses down from my wrist to my elbow. I loved the way his eyes sparkled when he noticed my smile. This dragon was going to be trouble for me, even after tonight's rituals.

Valk seemed to have a desire to memorize every small curve of my body. Every inch of my form felt cherished. He'd promised worship, and I hated to admit it, but I was glowing.

He'd let me go, albeit begrudgingly, when I'd said I needed to check in on the mages and their preparations for the ceremonies tonight. I'd promised that I would see him one more time before tying myself to Eldates, but I think we'd both known that was a lie. With the day's arrival, time had begun to move so quickly.

I also couldn't escape Aedan forever. I needed to fill him in on the things I was willing to disclose about the evolution of my relationship with Valk and hope that it didn't enrage him. However, if Valk could hold my esper. . .it might be best for everyone. I just had to sell Aedan on the idea to not blood bond him to the mages. Perhaps with Valk watching out for me, I could avoid being in the path of Aedan's fury. Maybe we could all work as a true team.

I'd flown back to the volcano, partly surprised that Valk hadn't followed me, but my lover did look truly exhausted. He'd stayed up all day and would need his rest if the ritual had to proceed as planned. Eldates most likely saw me fly in, but I needed to talk to Aedan alone. I had precious little time to make any changes to the impending events.

Clusters of mages shuffled about as I raced down the hall towards the place where Aedan and I had been residing. The mages were no longer hiding their engorged numbers due to the timing of the upcoming ritual; all of them stopped to bow their heads as they parted, allowing me to pass.

Within moments, I stood in the rounded entryway to our temporary cavern. Darkness overwhelmed the space, and an angry energy threatened to boil over. But it didn't feel like Aedan's.

A low growl to my left resonated, bouncing off the rocky walls. Red eyes focused on me from the shadows. "Cenara. . . You are alive."

A soothing wash of relief overcame me as I recognized the deep voice. The shadow morphed and twisted, releasing screams into the mist while he took on the softer form we usually interacted in.

"I was just about to slaughter them all after I received father's message." Malice poured from his words, but through the toxicity, all I could hear was that he was worried for me.

My heart nearly burst from pure joy. I gave him my biggest smile and ran straight into his waiting arms. He towered over me by more than a foot and a half. "Cholios! What are you doing here? We haven't secured the land yet. Tonight. After tonight, everyone should be good to come here."

"You think I would be able to stay away if something had actually happened to you? No." Cholios snarled before he looked down at my beaming face. I couldn't even pretend to be scared of him. "I got his message and came as soon as I heard. The dragons aren't that important, not like you are."

"What did I tell you, son? Pets have a way of returning, no matter what your intentions are," Aedan sneered, watching me with calculated eyes. The way he sat back in his chair relayed just how unconcerned he'd been with the outcome of this scenario. He put up with me only because his son loved me.

"Valk let me use his fire to anchor myself through the day," I reported, almost a little too proudly. Being able to unbind from Aedan would be the biggest personal win. . .*If* I could pull it off somehow. "I found out what their treasures are and why we can't find them. They are scales buried in their chest cavities. I don't know if it's true because I'm not a dragon, but he says that the holder of the scale can't be denied by the dragon."

"So, you still don't have his?" Aedan commented with a shake of his head.

"I don't think I need to take Valk's to persuade him to join us. He wants to please me, and I think he understands how important you are to me," I said, looking up at my brother. "I think I can make him an actual ally. He's smart, thoughtful, and passionate."

"Cenara, we don't know them well enough to take that risk," Cholios chided. I frowned, knowing if he said no that I would obey no matter how my heart sank. He brushed the hair out of my eyes and studied my face. "You care for this dragon."

"I'm not asking for all of them, just him. He witnessed my efforts on Fursia, and now he is declaring that he will aid me, protect me. Your enemies are his." My voice came out in a plea, and he did me the courtesy of pretending to consider my request. "I don't care for him above what we need to do to make this safe for you. You know you are my everything. Just. . .if there's a chance to keep his mind whole, then please, can we? He's willing to bond and mate me tonight."

"Force him to fight for it." Aedan rose to his feet and leveled me with a stern look. "Eldates is the king, and we need you tied to the most powerful dragon. Will the other dragons follow Valk?"

"I honestly don't have any idea. They don't seem to really follow Eldates either. Will that even matter after the blood bonding?" I bit my lip as I thought about all the potential scenarios. I wanted to ask Aedan how exactly he wanted Valk to fight for it with the ritual starting so soon.

"If I can convince Eldates to concede to Valk as the king. . .could we change the ritual?"

Aedan and Cholios exchanged a glance over my head before my brother released a patient sigh. "If you have something in mind, then do it fast."

That was good enough for me and probably the only approval I would get on the matter. "Are you going to stay with us now?"

Cholios smiled with the depths of the darkness of his shadows. It terrified some of the people we encountered, but I knew what each smile meant. Something about this world excited him in a way I hadn't seen for decades. "Not yet. I will be here for the rituals after I provide the update to the others and then we will leave again. I have some things to wrap up, but I look forward to relocating here permanently. I have a good feeling about this planet."

"You mean it? Is this the one?" I'd been waiting to hear these words for centuries. We'd been moving for so long, and each place brought us closer to where we would set up an actual home base. It couldn't just be a coincidence that I found Valk and that this ended up being a perfect location to consider home. I wouldn't call it fate, but maybe something was written in the stars after all.

"The final pieces are all being moved into place." My brother's gaze turned far off into the distance to something I would never be able to see.

"She lives then." I vocalized the words that neither of them seemed to want to speak. The one destined to be the final champion. Once he conquered her. . .nothing would be able to stop us.

"Salixa has confirmed it from the gamayun. The other immortals are in a frenzy to mask her location, but I will find her. Until then, we stay the course, starting with the dragons."

Aedan leaned back with a cruel smile of his own, but I could only nod at my brother. If I understood him correctly, then we might be looking at our actual home. If I did my part, then we'd never have to run again. If I did everything perfectly. . .perhaps Valk could remain at my side, and as Cholios grew his strength for the final challenge, I could be free of this curse.

A dark portal grew behind Cholios, and he nodded to his father before his bright red eyes fell back to me. "Keep your guard up. You remember what happened with the last dalliance and how he broke your heart."

"Yes, but then you ate his, and I haven't thought about him a day since then." I shrugged off the faceless man from my memories. He was nothing like Valk, but I couldn't convince them of that with so little time to prepare. "I will deliver the dragons to aid our mission. For you. I promise to never lose myself to a distraction like that again."

He leaned down and kissed the top of my head. "Of all the people who could betray me, I do not doubt your loyalty."

I beamed under his adoration until he vanished into the screaming portal. I never got to see the end result of us fleeing a planet anymore. He was too protective of me for that. I wasn't immortal like they all were. I'd had my wings and flame broken more times than I could count, so desperate our enemies became in their final struggles. Each time that happened, Cholios responded with a force that ended up wiping out more acolytes than intended, setting us back.

After the last time, Salixa insisted that Aedan and I cleared the way for our new temporary home. His fire and mine made the task easier to persuade the desires of those we encountered. Sometimes Brenden joined us. I always preferred that, but it wasn't up to me. For Cholios, I would endure Aedan. My brother was going to change the universe when he ascended to his rightful place and destroyed those false gods.

Once the swirl closed, I sighed and turned on my heel to find Aedan watching me with a look that made me wary.

"You were with Valk the whole time?"

"Yes. You just let him take me!" My voice flirted with the boundary of a shout before I dropped my gaze. I did not want to get hit again right now, especially when he had equal blame. Why did I feel the need to defend myself in this instance? He could have stopped it before it had happened and yet he'd chosen to do nothing.

"You are more than capable of getting away from him if you wanted to."

I hated the way he called me out, but he wasn't wrong. "His mountain has this raging storm surrounding it. I was waiting for an opening to return after I found the treasure, but one never came. Then he told me that he controls the storms around that particular mountain."

"If he is willing to mate you, why didn't he give you the treasure?" Aedan mused as a cluster of mages came through the room to gather candles from him that had been blessed by Salixa. "That was a giant risk for you to take with your life. When you didn't return for the daylight, I wondered if we'd lost an asset."

An asset. Naturally. I knew Aedan wouldn't show any care beyond how it might impact my brother. I'd known I would have to face Aedan's wrath for being late but to know Cholios had come himself. Well, even the beast in front of me couldn't cool the warmth of love in my soul.

"He will give it to his mate. I have made no promises to him in that regard, but he knows I want it. There's a chance that he is trying to persuade me with the treasure."

I pulled the strand of my shadow magic to open a mini portal where I kept my own personal things. Using both hands, I lifted Salixa's hefty book of shadows out and hugged it to my chest.

"You've never considered a mate until now. Never even mentioned it," Aedan pointed out, catching my eyes again. "There are perks to having a mate bond with the dragons, but the blood bond will suffice in keeping them under our control. Think carefully before you tie yourself indefinitely on a whim."

"How long did it take before you knew she was the one?" I asked, though perhaps it was too casual for our dynamic. None of them discussed how they'd come to find one another.

To my surprise, he weighed out a response. "I've always been suspicious and angry with everyone in my life, except my brothers. I was the same with her when she appeared."

For a moment, he fell silent, but I could tell that he wasn't done with this answer. His eyes had traveled to something that I could not see and didn't want to interrupt.

"Brenden and Declan were besotted with her after one evening, but I had some issues to work out. My inner beast revealed himself while I claimed her. We became obsessed. And now? She is the only thing to temper my anger."

"You weren't a dragon before you met her?" My fingers gripped the book tighter. I didn't bother to hide my shock. How could I have not noticed before?

"No. My brothers and I are something more powerful than beasts. We are changelings; our kind are almost as rare as yours. Bringing me back to my point. A dragon bond is a powerful tool, and he will be unable to hurt you with the obsession it promises. But you need to evaluate whether that is enough for one such as you. Cholios cherishes you, and while I don't always understand it, you are tied to our family. Make Valk earn a mating call to you."

That was the highest compliment he could have given me. Between the sentimental gift of Salixa's book, Cholios' unexpected visit to check on me, and Aedan's almost fatherly advice, I felt the desire to pinch myself to make sure I wasn't actually dreaming.

"It's time to make an appearance before the ritual. You and Eldates are first." Aedan snapped his fingers, and just like that, any sweet moment we might have had was gone. It was Aedan after all. "You have about an hour to figure out how to handle the beasts. I suggest you make good use of your time, or the plan remains intact. Make sure to wash Valk's scent off your skin thoroughly or there will be trouble."

I felt all the blood rush from my face as I stumbled over nothing. *One hour to change everything.* The only way I could change the course of the evening was to get ahold of Eldates' scale. And that was a lot more intimate than I wanted to get. For Valk, I had to try. . . But for Cholios, I would accept my fate if I wasn't fast enough.

CHAPTER 18 – CENARA

Salixa's tome flipped straight to the page for cleansing and restoring my body for the ritual ahead. Aedan was right, I couldn't approach Eldates marked by his brother, but removing Valk's scent from my skin hurt more than I expected. Using my magic, I wove a new dress made of fiery colored feathers and then wrapped my mage's cloak around me. Just enough to tease a peek of my legs and the tops of my breasts but also appear official. Exactly as I had on our arrival.

I hastened my steps down the hall towards the floating pavilion where I heard shouting. What could possibly be happening now?

"I believe I was very clear when I said that she wouldn't have any mages!" Lawry growled at Aedan. The fire dragon was nose-to-nose with our leader, heat emanating from his bare chest.

Three mages stood on the other side of Aedan as close as they could get to Izotza without provoking the other dragon further. Blood dripped down one mage's arm.

"All of you will be participating in the blood ritual. I understand that she is your only female dragon currently, and that makes you defensive, but there will be more." Aedan's words came out in a cool, harsh tone that I only heard because I'd moved closer.

Eldates didn't look particularly interested in engaging on either side, but he gave me that charming smile as I appeared in his line of vision on the other side of Aedan.

"There could be a hundred other female dragons for all I care! That won't change the fact that I am saying not a single one of your mages will touch this one." Lawry snapped at him, somehow managing to maintain his soft form even though scales flickered across his body.

Izotza stood three feet away from Lawry, her eyes caught in a feral beast slit as she watched the two men. A soft sound caught my attention, and I realized that I could hear her chest purring. It sounded different from Valk's, but the intent had to be the same. It was an attempt to soothe her lover. The female dragon might be too close to nesting.

"Aedan, let's change plans for tonight," I started smoothly, waiting for him to give me his attention before I continued. "Izotza needs to be matched with only female mages, but also, I believe we should postpone the blood ritual for her until after Lawry is assured that it won't hurt her. Last thing we need tonight is feral dragons and dead mages."

"Does that sound fair to you? That way, you can see how harmless the ritual is?" Aedan asked of the dragon stalking his every movement. There was a delay effect with the mind warping that wouldn't take effect until the next time they slept, so none of the men would be the wiser to what had happened. I was pretty confident we could handle Izotza if she were about to breed.

Izotza stepped up and wrapped her body around one of Lawry's arms as only she could likely do in this moment without starting a fight. The purring grew louder, and Lawry gave a subtle nod. He finally allowed Izo to pull him away from Aedan.

"I don't want to blood bond with any mages either!" The tall, skinny poison dragon shouted in what sounded more like a whine. When Aedan turned to look his way, he shrunk down to not appear challenging.

I raised an eyebrow at Eldates, waiting for him to take charge of this situation, but again, nothing happened. He just shook his head and looked disgusted.

Clearing my throat softly, I stepped in between the dragon and Eldates. "I'm sure there are a lot of nerves about tonight. Eldates and I will go first and show you all there is nothing to fear. The blood bond makes us loyal to one another, we offer you our powers, you offer up your strength and protection. It makes our energies symbiotic. That's all this is."

Looking him over again, I wasn't exactly sure what strength we would get from this particular dragon, but maybe upon discovery of the feral side of his nature, it would emerge.

"I don't want your power. I want to be left alone," he snarled my way with a mouth full of teeth. Interesting. Maybe there was a little bite in him after all.

Eldates wrapped an arm around my waist, guiding my body against his. It took everything in me to not shudder at the repulsion to his touch. "Velenu, this is happening. You aren't nesting like Izo is. This will be done for all of us tonight. If you need a final moment to yourself, go find my lazy brother. He's still not here, and I won't be disobeyed tonight of all nights."

Velenu growled low in his chest but then sulked away down the trail towards the exit of the pavilion.

When I turned my gaze back to him, the king of dragons gave me his dashing smile that likely would have wooed any normal woman. I couldn't deny his attractiveness; I just couldn't shake the blaze that Valk had set in every inch of my being. I used my best practiced smile in return before twisting my body around in his arms. He meant to use me and then discard me from the way that Valk spoke. Looks like we were both playing the same game, but I knew I would come out on top either way.

"There are a few last things we need to discuss before this ritual. Is there somewhere private on this pavilion?" I asked, leaning closer and resting my hand on his chest.

Eldates placed his hand over mine, catching my fingers. He tilted his head to indicate a corner hidden behind pillars. I followed him, trying to mask the urgency in my step as the moments ticked by.

"I heard you left with Valk last night," Eldates rumbled against my ear. Thick, heavy drapes fell from the awning above the pillars, and with a flick of my wrist, I manifested a lantern to bring us out of the darkness. "I was surprised when you didn't return. That you missed all the rest of the plans. Aedan didn't seem to be concerned with it, but should I expect you to just vanish for hours at a time after tonight?"

I considered my words carefully. Valk had mentioned to Aedan that he wanted to mate me. Had he said the same to

Eldates? "We had to have a frank conversation about some of the entitlements he felt with regard to our arrangement. Unfortunately, I'd not been prepared to be snatched up in some strange dragon ritual."

Eldates threw his head back and laughed so loud that I was sure everyone could hear him. "Yeah, that is a pretty typical dragon thing."

"Well, we seem to be able to have a conversation without a snatching, so that's something. As to my disappearances, you know that I do return to the rest of my family to aid where I can. I was thinking that in the future, you might come with me." My words grew soft, and I looked away, feigning bashfulness at being so bold to invite him along.

"If it's part of your mages' responsibilities, I don't see why I shouldn't be there. The mages are a bit chaotic; they will need a firm hand to direct them." His finger tips grazed my hips under my cloak, and a soft groan tore from his throat. "Your curves are so tempting. Your form is nothing like a dragon's."

I had to allow it. I had to let him touch me for the next part to work. I didn't bother to inform him that my mages would never listen to him because he'd be nothing more than a beast when he awoke next. A beast under my persuasion. If I could just get his scale. . .I'd have him switch with Valk. If I gave Valk a chance to accept Cholios, there was a chance he wouldn't have to become nothing more than a powerful tool. He could be at my side; he could be mine, truly.

"Is that something you like?"

"I'm dying to find out." His voice was husky, his hand slipping along my shoulder under my cloak. He groped my ass with his free hand, pulling me up to his body and against his chiseled chest. "I don't know how you managed to keep him off of you during the snatching, but this can be just another thing he'll never have."

"We will have plenty of time after the ritual tonight," I promised. Sadly, that part was true because until he fell asleep, I would have to endure him.

"A quick test right now would go a long way to taming my beast before the ritual. When you draw blood, it spikes our fury; having my scent on you would make this easier."

He was baiting me.

But I couldn't argue; it sounded reasonable for dragons.

"Valk offered me something," I teased, just to see how obsessed he might be with one-upping his brother. "He said that it would mark me as his if I wore it, that dragon law wouldn't let you even touch me. Is this something I should have on me during the ritual?"

Lies. All of it was lies, but would he go along with it?

Eldates raised an eyebrow at me and thought for a moment. "He offered *you* his scale? And you didn't take it?"

"Why would I take his scale if I'm meant to be with you?" I asked innocently. He didn't need to know that I absolutely would have taken the scale if Valk had truly offered it to me. I might have regretted it later, but I was an act first, question things later kind of gal.

"Did you kill him?" Eldates asked me out of the blue.

I frowned at him.

"What?" I knew my face looked genuinely shocked because I hadn't seen that question coming. "No, of course not. You are to be our partners. Why would I kill my allies even if they are obsessed with me?"

He grabbed my arm roughly, just past the point of uncomfortable pain. "Because if he is obsessed enough to offer you his scale, then he wouldn't just let you fly away. That's not how it works with dragons."

Well, shit. I should have seen that coming. "I didn't just fly away. We had a long conversation about how he feels and why I don't feel the same. I think the poor guy is heartbroken which is why he's not here right now. You'll see when Velenu returns. But if I had *your* scale, wouldn't that prevent any fighting between you two since you would clearly be my choice?"

Eldates considered me for a moment, and I could see a decision warring behind his eyes. He released my arm and took a seat on the long bench in the space with us. "This is how it will be done then. I want to see every single curve, and then, while you take a turn on my lap, I will show you how to access it. With my scale and my seed, Valk will be forced to fall into line. You will return the scale after the ritual once he has settled down."

My stomach twisted into a knot. I'd never give him the scale back. But would Valk accept me after I'd been with Eldates, even if it was only to get my hands on his scale to make my lover the king? This was quite a tangle I'd locked myself into. I hated the way the dragon smirked when I hesitated.

Coming to a decision, I let the cloak fall from my shoulders. I'd beg for forgiveness later so long as Valk retained his mind. If I didn't do this, he'd be lost to the beast forever, and none of it would matter.

Why did I have to care about Valk so much? If this weren't an issue, then only the blood bond would be necessary. But because I cared for him. . .I was trapped.

I kept my face calm and seductive despite my inner turmoil. Eldates didn't need to know that I struggled with what he asked of me. Slowly, I began to undo the few buttons on the top of my dress. The material sagged, and it took everything in me to not

187

cover my breasts when it fell open. The tension in the space grew thick as my hand slid for the tie.

"Come closer," Eldates growled. I took a shaky step forward and prayed he didn't notice my hesitation in the dimly lit privacy. His chest rippled with scales, a red glow illuminating the outline of each one.

I'm doing this for the scale. I'm doing this for the scale. I repeated the mantra over and over as the first tie unraveled and the fabric fluttered to the floor. Gods, I hated this.

Valk, please forgive me.

CHAPTER 19 – VALK

My senses alerted me that someone had entered my domain. I'd only had a short while to rest after Cenara left to prepare for the ritual. *Oh, fuck. That was tonight.*

"Who the hell is here?" I snarled, untangling myself from the sheets that still smelled like my little bird.

"It's me again," Velenu growled in a tone that was highly unusual for him. "I'm not doing it. I refuse to blood bond. He can't make me. She can't force this. You have to stop it."

I tied my linen back into place while fighting off the grogginess. "Did you tell them that?"

"Yes, but I need you to stand up to them. Even though it's obvious now that she may have gotten to you too."

"What do you mean 'too?'" I focused my glare at the insinuation I was behaving the same way Eldates had been.

"This rash behavior on your part hasn't changed anything! This blood bond is more than it seems, and we are heading straight into a trap. Eldates is ready to dive headlong into it for more power, but I'd rather cut ties now and go off on my own. I was sent to retrieve you, but we could just bolt now." His eyes pleaded with me to agree. Dragons in hordes often didn't need companions, but I'd never heard of an instance where a dragon split from their horde unless it was for a mating bond.

"Hey. You know I won't let them force you. I agree that the blood bonds seem suspicious. If Eldates wants to do it so badly, then he can tie himself to their mages, but we need to be there to support him in case he changes his mind." I splashed a bit of water on my face and then gestured for the exit. The storm outside had been quiet while I slept just in case she returned, but with the ritual, of course, she wouldn't have come back.

"We can't do anything about her. . ."

Cenara. I couldn't let her bond to Eldates. I'd almost slept past it by accident; then there would truly have been nothing that could be done. "I will deal with Cenara. Come on. We need to fly fast."

Velenu and I landed on the platform after only a short flight through a relatively calm night sky. I ran over every way to approach this situation, but in the end, I couldn't predict how my brother would respond to what I was about to do.

The main caverns were quiet, but chatter came from the volcanic pavilion. We followed the voices. I walked past all the altars that had been set up for tonight. Izotza and Lawry were tangled together in one corner of the landing, and I was glad to see that they'd made up enough to stop fighting. Sutenar was standing but bound to an altar on my left, snarling at the mages who got close to him. Otror sat to the side of another altar with a somber look of defeat on his face that seemed to echo Velenu's.

I felt Aedan's eyes on me before I spotted him. They shimmered red in challenge, but the smirk spoke of his amusement. "Valk, so glad you could join us. We were worried you would miss everything."

"I'm sure you were, Aedan. Where is my brother? I need to talk with him. *Alone.*" I emphasized the last word to make sure he knew I wasn't messing around. He may have kicked my ass two days ago, but I wouldn't cower to him.

"He's with Cenara just over there." Aedan gestured with his right hand and stepped out of my way as I went to pass him.

Perhaps it would be better for the three of us to talk together. "Velenu, stay here, I will make this work." I didn't wait for his response before throwing back the drapes shielding this portion of the pavilion and striding in.

The space was lit with only a few candle lanterns, and it took a moment for my eyes to adjust.

"Valk. . ." Cenara whispered. From the fractured way she spoke my name, I could tell that she was distressed.

Eldates' glowing red chest caught my attention first. Then my eyes found her. My precious phoenix was attempting to cover herself, her dress hanging partially open. Tears rolled down her cheeks, catching the light on their free fall.

"You aren't supposed to. . . Valk, I can ex—" she started to say before Eldates cut her off.

"Brother, get out of here. She's chosen me, and I won't discuss the matter with you further." He waved a hand at me as if I could be dismissed that easily.

Mine.

Cenara was mine.

I swallowed hard, fighting against the pain that tore at my insides, demanding to be set free. My beast picked up on the shift in her posture immediately; she didn't want him to touch her, but she'd put herself in this situation. It wasn't hard to put the pieces together about why now, before the ritual. I'd told her exactly what it was and what it did. She was still chasing after the damn treasure so she could make him stand aside for me. I would deal with that after.

Then he made the mistake of reaching out to touch her.

My roar rattled the entire pavilion, shaking the pillars of the volcano. Fury sped down my body. Lightning ripped out of me, shredding the drapes and coursing into the night sky. I began to shift as I leapt for him and caught him by the neck with my scaled hands. We toppled over the bench and the edge of the pavilion towards the lava below.

"Valk!" Cenara screamed, but I didn't turn to look at her. Anger surged through every fiber of my being, demanding that I kill him for touching what we all knew to be mine. I strangled him, squeezing until he punched me in the soft tissue of my gut.

"Are you insane?" Eldates growled before our transformations took over. His words were barely perceptible over the wind rushing past in our descent. Our wings broke free, catching our free fall. I banked right with a charged blast of lightning tearing from my throat. He pivoted up, and I followed him out of the volcano, catching the drift with furious beats of wings.

"You'll never be good enough to beat me. Even she picked me. All you had to do was wait, you impatient idiot."

He dared to taunt me now? Flashes of his hand on her flesh turned my vision red. Lightning struck again, just missing him as he flew away towards the brewing storm. Eldates charged up the fire in the core of his chest, diving at me from above. His claws sliced sideways. I narrowly avoided an injury to my left wing as I pulled it out of the way.

With a snarl, I gave chase through the eastern mountain peaks, avoiding clusters of jagged rocks as my lightning rippled in the sky above, waiting for my command. Plumes of night mist rose from the icy waters below, and I flew once more into the darkness. His red glow gave him away. I wouldn't let him escape me.

"I shine brighter than you ever could," he continued, amusement layering his words. *"I'm larger and more powerful than you. The world needs me and disregards you. Why would they want pyrite when they could have gold?"*

I could pretend the words didn't sting, but my ego knew better. I'd avoided this confrontation my whole life because I didn't want to find the truth in his words.

Fire burst around me in a tight circle. I twisted, flying straight up into the sky, avoiding his strike. Caught in the fiery whirlwind, flames spun around me. I dodged the scorching whips lashing out, emerging through the top miraculously unscathed. Balls of fire shot out in every direction, catching the land beneath us on fire. In the darkness of night, it looked like an ocean of flames.

Eldates charged at me from below, and we locked claws, tumbling over one another mid-flight. *"One thing I don't understand, Brother. I said you could have her when I was done. If you obeyed. Why choose to die this way? There was so much power for you and lands of your own, yet you choose this?"*

Words lost their meaning; this was the way of the old lands we'd lived on.

A cluster of lightning wrapped around us. The electric shocks didn't hurt me, but Eldates roared, exposing his neck. I took advantage and chomped down at the base of his jugular, sinking my teeth as deep as they would go. Without a second thought, I ripped the softer flesh and scales out.

Instead of releasing me, his claws sank in. Pulling me close, thick blood coating us, he turned us towards the ground in what was known as a death spin. Twisting, turning, warping to the wind, we plummeted.

"Valk!" Cenara's scream flooded my mind as the hurricane winds blazed past.

The ground rushed up to meet us both. I only had a few moments to act. Eldates' grip on me wavered as the lethal neck wound drained his energy. I twisted, trying to pry myself from his grip, but his back talon had pierced through the scales and one of my wings was stuck. Using my other wing, I attempted to rotate us as the rocky cliff came into view. The only way to survive the impact was to use his body as a shield.

His heavy breath was the only warning. . .

He released a plume of fire from his mouth and the gaping hole in his neck, hitting me directly in the face. The burn sizzled against my scales, but I didn't have enough time to react.

The wall of stone met us head-on.

"I hope you die with me for your treachery." Eldates' declaration was weak, his voice wheezy.

The world exploded. Fire, stone, and speed collided.

Then everything faded to black.

CHAPTER 20 – CENARA

"I believe this matter has been resolved," Aedan mused in my mind. He'd been laughing since Valk attacked Eldates and they both fell over the edge. He didn't seem concerned in the slightest that we might have lost two dragons!

Seeing my dark dragon soar into the sky after his brother, I'd immediately shifted. I hadn't cared that it was supposed to be Valk's fight. If joining forces would have helped him come out on top, then I would do it. Aedan seemed to have read my mind and had trailed after me, absorbing me in the shadows when I'd gotten too close.

Now, the shadow dragon watched from the top of a nearby cliff as we waited for fire, smoke, and dust to clear. How could any beast survive a fall like that? Why Eldates would even use a move like that was beyond me.

I wanted to call for Valk, but my voice stuck in my throat. What if he didn't want to hear from me? What if he didn't live but Eldates did? A million more 'what ifs' rolled around in my head, but all I could do was hover in the air, flapping my wings nervously, waiting for the dust to settle.

It took a few moments, but as the wind pushed away the haze, I breathed again.

A black dragon—with specks of pyrite like the ones that marked the skin I knew so intimately—emerged. A song came out of my heart in the form of chirps and whistles as I flew towards him. Aedan didn't move to stop me.

"Bring him to our side now," Aedan demanded before he spread his wings and flew off in the direction of the volcano to rejoin the others. *"I expect you back to complete the rituals."*

"I will," I promised absently. I just wanted to be closer to Valk. Nothing else mattered right now.

Valk's eyes tracked my every movement as I flew the span between us and circled around him in the sky. There weren't any great places for me to land; the landslide left a few piles that balanced precariously on the new surface. I picked the one that looked the most stable, tucked my wings in at my side, and locked eyes with him.

My dragon responded with a growl, his tail whipping around in agitation. He didn't seem to be welcoming my presence at all, but I couldn't stay away from him. I couldn't keep back any longer.

I'd beg for forgiveness if he needed me to. I hadn't wanted it to come to this. How would he deal with the death of his brother? Would he be mad at me? Blame me for the game we all knew had been played? I would deal with his wrath if he would just let me be close to him.

"Valk. . ." I didn't bother hiding the sorrow from my voice. I didn't want to fight with him, but it might be unavoidable. Lightning tore through the sky above me, keeping my nerves on edge.

"Shift," Valk demanded, keeping me pinned with a glare.

I complied immediately.

With slow steps, I climbed over the terrain, inching myself within striking range. With my mage magic, I could disappear if he attacked, but I refused to be scared of him. Not when my heart sang this way. In his arms, I would be safe—with my heart, with my body, with my life. I knew this to be true even if I didn't know how.

His dragon scented me, and a new snarl tore from his throat before he shifted down. Valk's eyes were tightly closed as he paced in front of me, working through his rage.

"You removed my scent and, in its place. . .left his. Did you choose him?"

The words were conversational, stated as matters of fact without even a hint of the fury that I could feel between us.

"No. I would never have chosen him, Valk." I kept my eyes locked on his face so that he would see how serious I was if only he would look at me again. "I had to—"

"Then why is his scent on you?" he roared.

It took everything I had not to shake; the ground trembled in its own response.

I took a step forward with bravery I didn't know I had and grabbed his face to make him look at me. "Because I needed his scale to make you king. I couldn't lose you to the ritual."

His anger faded before my eyes, the meaning of my words sinking in. "You wanted to blood bond to me instead, and this was the only way."

"No. I want so much more than that with you." My hand fell from his face to the center of his chest, between all those beautiful pyrite markings. I smiled as the rhythm of his heart quickened.

"Cenara," he whispered, caressing my cheek, his other arm pulling me in closer. "Mine."

"Yours," I confirmed in a purr. There was nothing more to say as we stared into each other's eyes, searching for anything other than love. Any hint of hesitancy, regret, or confusion.

My heart knew that Valk had changed absolutely everything for me. I was free to live in a world where I could defend my brother but also experience all that this dragon promised. After tonight, if he came with me, then no one would separate us, and I'd give him all that I was asking for in return.

Valk tilted my head up so that our lips crashed together, erasing the mark of the dragon who lay still in the rubble of the landslide a hundred yards away. There wasn't any lingering rage, and from what I could see, there hadn't been any sadness at the passing of his brother. I'd have to wait to find out how this moment might come back to haunt me in the end. It couldn't be over that easily.

"Fly with me." Not quite a question, even if his words were soft against my lips.

"Always," I said as we stepped apart to transform into our beasts.

He launched into the sky and caught the draft spinning around me. I followed his movements to catch the same current, lifting me so that we were beside one another as if a magnet attached us together.

Mirroring each other, the tips of our wings brushed, despite his longer wingspan. Each turn along the gusts enhanced the sound of his purring. It reverberated in my chest, in my heart, setting us to the same rhythm. Every movement bonded my spirit to his in a way that I would have sworn was impossible before this evening.

"My heart, my spirit, my essence are yours. You are the only treasure that will ever matter from this day forward." Valk's promise wove its way through the air as if a magical tether would seal the union. He turned once more, and I rode the gust with him into the starry sky. *"Your dreams, your hopes, and your fears are mine. You will never walk this world, or any other, alone. You will always know that you are loved. This is the vow I make to you, my dragon's mate."*

CHAPTER 21 – VALK

Cenara made the most beautiful sounds, her joy at our bonding evident. My chest warmed with heat that wasn't from my own lightning glow. It was the flame of her heart, the one beating in rhythm with mine. She'd chosen me to stand beside her, to fly alongside, and to protect her from the dangers in the life she'd lived prior.

But now there were other things to address, things I'd noted that she'd said in previous conversations.

With Eldates gone, I needed to do what he hadn't been able to fight against. I wasn't after power like he was. It was time to renegotiate with Cenara's family.

I landed smoothly and watched my mate land beside me. She nuzzled against my neck and side with her soft, pillowy form before shifting back into the smaller, curvy form that riled up my beast. Bones crunched while I shrank down in size to walk beside her. My fingers slipped into hers, and she offered me a bright smile.

"I guess it's time for the rituals, though some changes will have to be made now that we are mated." Cenara hummed in thought before she bowed her head to the cluster of mages that we walked through. "I need to get you one of Salixa's potions to help enhance your recovery."

"Hold off on that for now," I said under my breath, noting the location of the other dragons in my horde. Sutenar and Lawry were snarling at Aedan, but I couldn't hear them just yet. "I may not be done fighting."

"All the more reason to heal you!" she protested, worry taking over that beautiful face of hers.

I only replied with a shake of my head. The others would need to see proof of the fight.

Every face turned our way as we finished crossing the bridge onto the platform. I bared my chest proudly to display the series of markings on my bare chest that told them all I was a mated dragon. Cenara didn't bat an eye at the hostile glances tossed her way from the other dragons as they worked out what this meant for them. She'd likely fight beside me no matter what I said if I had to take on both of the fire dragons.

"I have defeated Eldates in combat. Are there any here amongst our horde who want to dispute my claim?" I snarled, keeping my voice from rising to a shout. Even though we'd never had a history of fighting one another, I couldn't be sure if any of them would challenge me.

To my surprise, Velenu stepped forward and met my eyes. "That depends on your next actions. If I'm to give up my freedom, I'd rather die here. . .fighting you."

Confusion and tension hung in the air between us. This was the old way of our people, the way we'd lived before coming here to this new land. Power used to change hands for no reason other than a talon slipping over another's border. We'd become complacent and weak with our lack of drive. Myself especially. Tonight, I would change that.

"Fair enough. The time for sitting by and letting the world pass us is over. Aedan, Cenara, and their mages have come to ask us for aid in their god's battle." I prefaced the conversation to my horde, but it was also directed at Aedan. "We can be pawns, or we can be power players. What do you choose? I know what my decision will be, but I will have yours. Then we can move forward."

Aedan raised an eyebrow to me as he sorted out what exactly I had discovered. Yes, I'd figured it out while I rested after Cenara left me. She was originally after our scales to control us into fighting for her brother. This blood ritual would strip away our ability to deny them, which is why she'd not demanded mine the night prior but went after Eldates. Her casual mention of losing me to the ritual was the final red flag about what was to come.

I understood why she was fighting after I experienced what she gave up every day. She needed them to survive, and if her god won, then her curse would be lifted. If they needed dragons, well, then she would have dragons, but it would be on *our* terms with all the facts laid out.

"I will fight." Izotza spoke first, and the four men snapped their heads to study her quick response. "I'd rather have a seat at the table than be ordered around. If you intend to fight alongside your mate, then I will fight with you."

Lawry kept his gaze on the tiny ice woman and nodded his agreement. "If change is upon us, then I choose to be part of what comes next."

"Sutenar?" I asked the fire dragon glowering in the corner.

"I'm in, but I want my powers back," he snarled at Aedan. Smoke poured from his nostrils, but it was devoid of any heat.

"Don't kill my son's mages or your allies, and you can have them back," Aedan agreed. He must have sensed the direction this was turning. When the dragon puffed out his agreement, Aedan merely snapped his fingers, sending flames coursing around the room and returning to Sutenar's chest.

The two poison dragons looked between each other. Velenu wasn't built for fighting, but he was a strategist. With his book knowledge, I had no doubt he'd make inspired changes to amplify the efforts of the acolyte recruitments. Otror, on the other hand, was toxic to the environment if he needed to be.

When they both nodded, I knew I had everyone on board. They were following in step behind me, showing me that they trusted I would take care of them. Now I needed to reward that trust.

I turned my attention to Aedan. He met my gaze with more interest than I'd seen from him in the past. "There you have it. However, there will be some changes to the original terms. We will fight with you as allies in your quest to reclaim the heavens for your god. We will act as free agents with no blood bonding unless *we* decide that is what we want to do in the future. Cenara will be acknowledged as my mate, and I will be the only one to care for her esper until the curse is lifted. Where you send her, I will go. The rest of our group will always be sent in pairs until we build up our own teams to have our backs in new lands."

"I can agree to all of these terms with one minor shift on our end," he countered easily, and I could see the dragons relax in my peripheral. "You will come with us now to prove your willingness to be our partners and then before the sun sets tomorrow you will vow your loyalty to our god. If you do that, then you can remain an independent unit. How does that sound?"

"I think we can make that work." I cast another glance at my horde before I amended. "If it doesn't work out with any of them or they don't wish to continue on this path, then I will be the one who decides how to proceed with them as part of my horde."

Aedan rubbed his chin thoughtfully, tossing a considering look to the high priestess at my side. I felt the weight of her gaze on me, but I held my head high. I wouldn't let them execute or force any of my people into blood bonds against their wills, and I didn't think she would make me.

"You have my agreement to these terms." The shadow dragon strode forward, and we clasped arms, flame, and smoke, forging the new terms of the deal on the table. "Let it begin then."

"Scissura," Cenara whispered and snapped her fingers. In the center of the platform, a large sphere manifested out of a ball of smoke. The edges crackled with power and a black energy that pulled all of us forward a bit. Through the glassy surface, fire and explosions erupted in the chaos of the night. Echoes of screams poured out like heavy gas, oozing along the bricks towards all of us gathered. "Impetum!"

The mages around us filed into three lines and leapt through the portal. My mate turned her excited gaze to me and then her and Aedan moved together. He stepped through first, a loud roar from his beast ringing back at us. Cenara turned to face me as she stepped backwards into the darkness.

"Together, my mate," she cooed at me, beckoning me with her fingers before she fell back and transformed.

"I won't force any of you," I started before noticing they were all beside me. I looked at each of their faces full of determination.

Velenu surprised me again when he answered first. "You have our hides; we will have yours. Let's go lock up this partnership."

In a matter of moments, all six of our beasts were flying into a new land erupting in chaos and violence. I turned on the wind towards the sound of my mate as she screeched her arrival on a town so large I couldn't see where it ended. Following in her wake, I took up a second line of my own. Lightning exploded out of me in every direction, leveling the eastern portion of the town.

Under the layers of screams, dark laughter followed me as I flew. The sound created a flicker of nervousness under my skin. But as I felt Cenara's heart respond to it with elation, I knew I wouldn't have any doubts ever again.

"We're going to turn this front around!" Cenara sang in my mind. *"It's all because of you. . ."*

Mine. *"Anything for you."*

I smiled internally as I landed on the ground amongst pillars of flames and swiped my large paw at a group of soldiers running away from my mate's power. I caught one in my mouth and shook until I heard that satisfying crack. Tossing the body into the shadows, the laughter drew closer, and the darkness appeared to move in sync. Not for the first time, I wondered if I signed up with the wrong side. In the end, it would change nothing. I had Cenara, my mate. And because of that, I would do it all over again.

I took a knee and the others followed suit behind me while the other mages gathered around our small group. The man in front of us exuded a darkness that was beyond imaginable. Where he stood, the light from the fire shriveled into nonexistence. Everything that passed him lost all warmth and hope, leaving behind only cold ferocity in its wake.

The fight had served its purpose of driving the common goal into all of us, what we were now a part of: the final rotation of a planet that had denied their god. We were the deliverers of his final call; those who refused were sentenced to die. Cenara advised me that they were currently engaged in similar battles on fourteen worlds. They were beginning this process on Artemesia as their final home, infiltrating not just us but the fae as well. The more information I was given, the more I realized I should probably protest their efforts. But I just couldn't bring myself to turn against her.

The dark god cast his eyes over each of us. I knew the moment His sight was upon me from the scorch mark left in my soul. He waited for us to deliver our vows, so I cleared my throat to indicate that we were to begin in unison.

"With the guidance of the night to come until the permanence of the great beyond, we will not betray the oath we take this evening. Until she has fallen and the origins tremble, our mission will continue until the day we draw our last breath. Hail, Cholios!"

As the black mark crawled up my arm and without understanding the full extent of the words we were told to recite, I knew we were signing our souls over. The god smiled, but there was no warmth. He laughed, but it wasn't friendly. The mages were marked with blood and death, and we had just agreed to become partners in this battle amongst the gods.

Then she appeared behind the god as the sun set in an alluring array of bright yellows, reds, and oranges, and everything set itself back on the right path. She bowed her head respectfully to Cholios on the dais above us but then turned her head to give me a smile more dazzling than the sun I'd just turned away from.

Cenara's quick steps brought her into my arms as I rose from my knee to catch her.

The god watched me intently before His words echoed in my head. *"I will always be around. If you fail to protect her in the battles to come, know that your death will be swift. If you betray us, your soul will plead for perpetuity."*

A chill shivered down my spine, but I wasn't afraid. I didn't need the warning from Him. I already understood what I agreed to, even if the others only had a tiny glimpse. I would never hurt my mate or deter her from the fiery path that she must travel.

I met my lover's bright yellow eyes and touched my forehead to hers. "I love you."

Her small hum of approval matched the song in our hearts as they beat together, knowing that we were going to take on the universe.

When history speaks of this time on Artemesia, they will say that the fae king fell to the shadows first. But I would know the truth. I'd turned my back on the world that had given us solace because, at the end of it all, for her, I would render life as we knew it to ash. All so she could rise again.

EPILOGUE – CENARA

100 years later

A surprising thing began to happen the more I connected with Valk. While I used to spend the days in a state of virtual nonexistence, each year together, my esper grew stronger thanks to the passion in his heart's flame. He'd built up a tolerance to the pain over the first few months and began to push what he could give me. With the added strength, I regained consciousness during the day, even if I was still nothing more than a ghost on the land.

No one but Valk could see or hear me while the sun reigned supreme overhead, but at least I had him. It was as if I'd been given half my life back. During the day, I floated beside him as he handled tasks in my absence; it was like a true partnership. I had to admit, while my family had been skeptical of the dragons, none of the horde had looked back after making their vows.

"They are going missing down these tunnels," I urged my mate with a repeat of the conversation we'd been having all day.

"That's not my primary focus, little bird. We are down here to see how the infernals are responding to the sacrifices we've been giving them so that they can adjust to the atmosphere here," Valk replied with the patience of a true born leader. He only ever used this voice with me. I'd seen him and Aedan get into it more than a few times over the decades; those arguments were never as kind. The only one we didn't fight with was Keane.

"Well, I'm going down this tunnel to see if I can find them," I said, walking my invisible body in that direction to do what I wanted. He could handle the infernals by himself.

Infernals were the lesser beings forced to do our bidding when we took over a planet. Mages were at the top of the chart in the infernal setup, with mindless beasts made of shadow and darkness at the bottom. Many of them could shapeshift into whatever we needed, something that proved to be immensely helpful. And once they made a deal with Cholios, upon death they would return to us to do our work for the rest of eternity.

Right now, we'd offered them bodies of elves, dwarves, and orcs so they could begin to learn about the world. Our dark prison in the pits of this volcano was the most effective place for the infernals to tear apart a person for years, eating memories and body parts, which granted their understanding of our ways and the world around them. Given enough time, they figured out how to survive. I didn't need to be a part of that right now. What I did want was to discover why my mages were going missing down these tunnels.

"I'd rather you wait for me," Valk insisted, even though he knew I couldn't be argued with. He'd punish me later, though unlike with Aedan, I wasn't afraid of those interactions.

"I'll be right back," I called over my shoulder without looking back. My handsome dragon would watch me until I was out of sight, no matter what I said.

Even though I was invisible and more like a wisp than an esper in my current state, I still took each step with caution. I really didn't know what was killing them. At least, I assumed they were dead. If they weren't, then they were deserters, and Cholios would hunt them down to claim their souls for good. I didn't understand what the big deal was, this trade essentially gave them a second chance at life, but still some grew to resent this gift.

Ahead of me on the path were flashes of fire and clanking of metal against stone. Shouts of coordinated efforts for a battle, and then I heard one of our infernals roar. They shouldn't be out yet; they were still acclimating to the environment.

"Valk, we have a problem!" I shouted through our bond and charged forward to get a better look at the situation.

"I told you that you should have waited for me. Turn around, and we will check it out together," he replied immediately. My dragon hadn't managed to go too far in the opposite direction yet.

"I'm going in now."

"Of course you are. On my way."

I felt the sigh in my heart before the adrenaline of the fight around the corner forced me to hold my breath.

The infernal was one of the earliest creations. I could tell from the way the shapeshift hadn't gotten all the details right. The beast dragged arms too big for its frame. Its disfigured face snarled and spat at the group of attackers. Dwarves battled with the infernal as it flailed and struck out at them, squishing one against a boulder.

Before the infernal wrapped its scaly fingers around a second dwarf, a glowing red sword tore through the beast. It fell to the ground in sizzling pieces as the flesh cooked.

Moving closer to investigate the flaming sword's wielder, I stumbled. The woman looked straight up into my face with eyes burning like the most welcoming firepit on the coldest night of the year.

Her red hair was bound back out of her face. Crimson lines ran down the skin visible around her leather armor. The woman was a nymph, from what I could tell, but the power coursing through her energy told me that I needed to be on my guard.

"An esper?" the woman said softly, almost reverently. "No one has seen one since the great migration. You don't need to be frightened."

She sheathed her sword with a fluid movement. While I was still trying to figure out how she could see me, she approached. I looked down at my hands, which were normally a ghostly outline. Instead, I was greeted with flames! Flames I hadn't seen in more than three centuries.

"How. . ." I whispered, jumping back in surprise when the woman knelt in front of me.

"I promise you are safe. What's your name?" Her voice was calm and soothing, like the crackling of the flame in a hearth. The call to her fire sang to me like a breezy night flight.

"Cenara."

Valk's proximity calmed my racing nerves as the stunning warrior took my hand, caressing the flames without a single concern about the danger I might present. My fire skin burned brighter where we touched as if she fueled my being.

She closed her fingers around mine, and I lost my breath, knowing this touch completed the final piece of my cursed soul. It shouldn't have been possible.

Everything was perfect with Valk and now, nothing would be the same again.

My spirit needed them both. She might be the key to making me whole.

"What a beautiful name. Notos can protect you and any others you have hiding out in the wilderness. I can offer you that personally as their eastern border leader. My name is Minithe."

The End. . .for now.

Bound By Flame Collection:

To Keep an Emerald Rose - Elayna R. Gallea - April 5th

To Ignite a Pyrite Spirit - Callie Pey - April 12th

To Snatch a Gilded Laurel - Alex Callan and Angelica Babineaux - April 19th

To Spare an Opal Soul - River Bennet - April 26th

To Scorch a Quartz Thorn- Fleur Devillainy - May 3rd

To Hunt a Ruby Remedy - Jen Lynning - May 10th

To Wed an Obsidian Villain - Vasilisa Drake - May 17th

To Claim a Silver Curse - Isabella Khalidi - May 24th

To Embrace an Onyx Heart - Sirena Knighton - May 31st

To Ignite a Pyrite Spirit is set in a shared story timeline with all the rest of my books:

Here's the timeline:

<u>The Revolt of the Marked (Dark Fantasy series -TBD Release)</u>
The Lament of the Dendron (TBD) Book 1

To Make a Monster*
To Ignite a Pyrite Spirit*

<u>The Dryad Chronicles (Fantasy Romance Series)</u>
Daughter of Earth (April 30th, 2024) Book 1
Calling of the Grove (TBD) Book 2
Whispers of the Wind (TBD) Book 3
Summoning of the Flame (TBD) Book 4
Cursed*
Tides of Healing (TBD) Book 5

The Root of Fey Magic*
When the Veil Meets the Moon*

* can be read as a standalone
If there isn't a date. It means the book is out!!

Thank you for reading! If you enjoyed this, please leave a review.

About the Author:

Callie Pey is the steamy fantasy romance author responsible for The Dryad Chronicles. She loves fantastical worlds and epic stakes that embrace love in all its forms with a heavy dose of adventure. A current Austinite, she enjoys reading almost as much as writing, painting, and finding even the smallest moments to capture joy. With one completed series behind her, Callie is now embarking on two brand new series to come: A dark fantasy not for the faint of heart and a paranormal romance that will feature parts of Texas!

Keep up with her at:

www.calliepey.com

Printed in Great Britain
by Amazon